SCAR
GIRL

SCAR GIRL

A NOVEL

LEN VLAHOS

🌱 Carolrhoda LAB

MINNEAPOLIS

5-9-16

Carolrhoda Lab™
An imprint of Carolrhoda Books
A division of Lerner Publishing Group, Inc.
241 First Avenue North
Minneapolis, MN 55401 U.S.A.

For reading levels and more information, look up this title at www.lernerbooks.com.

Cover and interior photographs: Michael Frost (rocker girl); © Robert Kohlhuber/Moment/
Getty Images (crowd); © Guru 3D/Shutterstock.com (headphones).

Main body text set in Iowan Old Style 10.5/18.
Typeface provided by Bitstream.

Library of Congress Cataloging-in-Publication Data

Cataloging-in-Publication Data for *Scar Girl* is on file at the Library of Congress.
ISBN: 978-1-60684-607-0 (LB)
ISBN: 978-1-60684-608-7 (EB)

Manufactured in the United States of America
1 – BP – 12/31/15

For all the people with whom I played
music when I was younger.

And for my parents, for putting up with me
and with all the people with whom I played
music when I was younger.

AUTHOR'S NOTE

What follows are transcripts of the interviews I conducted with the Scar Boys over a period of five weeks—stretching from early February to late March 1989—while the band was in the studio recording the follow-up to their debut album, Minus One. Though this material has been edited and rearranged to make the story flow, all of the words attributed to members of the band are true and accurate.

Here, then, are the Scar Boys, in their own words. I hope you find their story as fascinating as I did.

Joanne Cryder
New York City, September 14, 1989

PART ONE.
JULY TO AUGUST 1986

We're a rock group. We're noisy,
rowdy, sensational, and weird.
—Angus Young

What defines you?

HARBINGER JONES

You mean aside from my face?

CHEYENNE BELLE

I guess I'd say that I'm not good at asking people for help.

RICHIE MCGILL

How the hell should I know? What defines you?

HARBINGER JONES

How much do you know about Johnny McKenna? He was the first singer in the Scar Boys. He, Richie, and I started the band together in the eighth grade. The whole thing was mostly Johnny's idea.

CHEYENNE BELLE

I didn't join the band until a year or two later. Some kid from their high school had been playing bass, but he quit.

At my first rehearsal, I remember that all three guys—Johnny, Harry, and Richie—were looking at me like I was from Mars, or maybe Venus. But the person who caught my eye most was Harry.

Harry had been struck by lightning as a kid, and he has all kinds of scars on his face, though they're not nearly as bad as he thinks. The lightning did a lot more damage inside than outside. Not like damage to his internal organs and stuff, but damage to his soul. Everything and everyone Harry sees in the world, he sees through the prism of a lightning bolt. All of us, all of this, lit up so bright that it gets distorted. He can't stand the light, so he hides in the darkness.

HARBINGER JONES

I wasn't struck by lightning. I was tied to a tree and the tree was struck by lightning. My injuries are the result of the severe burns I received when the tree caught fire. I was kind of like a marshmallow on a stick that gets too close to the flames.

Did Chey say I was struck by lightning?

You have to take Chey with a grain of salt. She likes to exaggerate the details of a story to make it better.

CHEYENNE BELLE

About a year after I joined the Scar Boys, Johnny and I started dating. He was after me from almost the first day. I kept saying no, that it would be bad for the band, but he kind of wore me down. Johnny was like that. He wouldn't stop until he got what he wanted. He had a kind of take-no-prisoners attitude, you know? I think that's what made me fall in love with him.

HARBINGER JONES

When we were on our first tour, the summer after we'd graduated high school, before there were tour buses and roadies, when it was just the four of us in the van, Johnny and I got into a big fight. It'd been bubbling under the surface for months. For me, the fight was about how I was Johnny's lackey, about how he was an emotional bully and I was an emotional cripple; it was even about our musical differences. But mostly it was about how I was in love with Cheyenne and how I hated that she was with him and not me. Johnny and I never said any of these things out loud; when you're close like we were at the time, all that unspoken stuff is just there in the room with you.

The fight got bad enough that I hit Johnny in the face. It was the first and only time in my life I ever hit another human being. The world had made me its personal punching bag for so long that I guess I finally lost it and punched back.

After I hit him, Johnny left the tour and went home, which, if you ask me, was a complete overreaction. We decided to continue on as a three-piece and even played one gig with me as the singer—it was this giant keg party in Georgia. It was probably the best night of my life. With Johnny gone and with that great show under our belts, I really thought it was the start of something special.

The next day was when we found out about Johnny's accident. There was nothing to do but give up the tour and go home.

You want to know what guilt is? Try punching—wait, strike that—try *slapping* your best friend in the face, and then watch as a chain of events unfolds that ends with him almost dying. I more or less shut down after that.

CHEYENNE BELLE

Johnny was hit by a car, about a mile from his house in Yonkers. They amputated his leg. Did you know they actually use a saw to do that? I mean a real saw. Do you think they buy them at the local hardware store or something? I can't even begin to imagine what that must've been like.

Anyway, Johnny wouldn't see me after the accident. I tried going to the hospital, tried calling his house, even tried just showing up. His mother kept running interference, but I knew Johnny was putting her up to it. He was pushing me away. It'd been almost a month since I'd seen him, and I was going out of my mind.

RICHIE MCGILL

The whole thing with Johnny's leg was fucked up. I was the only one in the band to visit him, and let me tell you, the dude was in bad shape. I mean, like, his hair was greasy and his clothes smelled and his room was a total mess.

He asked me why Harry didn't come, too, and I didn't know what to say. Harry had shut himself off from the rest of the world and was kind of being a whiny bitch. Johnny didn't need to hear about Harry's crap while he was sitting there with one of his legs gone.

I called Harry and tried to convince him to go see Johnny, but when that dude gets caught up in his own shit, there's no getting through.

I give him a pass, though, you know, because of his face and stuff.

HARBINGER JONES

Both Richie and my shrink got on my case about being a recluse after the tour imploded, but it wasn't until serendipity put Cheyenne and me in the same place at the same time that things changed.

I was on one of my favorite walking paths, feeling sorry for myself, blaming myself for what had happened to Johnny, when I stumbled across Chey standing on a footbridge. She looked so incredibly beautiful standing there that any thought of Johnny went right out of my head. I ignored every good instinct I had and decided to go for broke.

"Chey, I love you," I told her.

She threw up on my shoes.

For real.

It turned out that Johnny had been keeping Chey away, and the girl was so tortured over it that she got literally lovesick all over my sneakers. I felt bad enough for her that I stupidly offered to help her and Johnny reconcile. (If I'm being honest, I would've done anything to make Cheyenne Belle happy, to make her like me back, even if it made no sense.) Of course, that meant I would have to visit Johnny first.

Johnny and I had a lot of stuff to work through, but we managed it. We took what was left of our tattered friendship to the only place where it would have a chance to heal: music. We found peace and we found our friend-ship buried in the music. It always comes back to the music.

And I was true to my word. My visit opened the door for Johnny and Chey to get back together.

CHEYENNE BELLE

Johnny lived in a much nicer part of town than me. His neighborhood was called Colonial Heights; mine was called McLean Avenue. That's the name of the street I grew up on. My neighborhood wasn't cutesy enough to have a name like Colonial Heights. His street was lined with oak trees, and the houses had shrubs and fences protecting mowed lawns with dogs barking hello in the front yard. Mine was a scraggly street with low-rent retail, auto shops, and apartment buildings. We had dogs, too, but they were mostly pit bulls and Doberman Pinschers. So Colonial Heights was a different world than mine, still Yonkers, but a different world.

Johnny's house was three stories tall, with dark wood trim and all kinds of funky angles. It sat on a bend in the road on a supersteep hill; and he told me that at least once a year someone would crash a car through the bushes that lined the curb and wind up on his front lawn. That's crazy, because the spot where Johnny was hit by the car, about a mile away, was almost exactly like that.

Inside, the house was massive, too big for Johnny and his parents. His older brother, Russell, moved to New York City after graduating college, like five or six years earlier, but even if Russell had been living there, the house still would've been too big.

The coolest thing about the place was the sunken living room. Maybe that's not the right thing to call it, because it was too tall to be sunken. Maybe I should just call it the cathedral, like Harry does. Floor to ceiling it was eighteen feet. I know that because Johnny liked to tell people that his was the only house that could hold a seventeen-foot Christmas tree and still have room for the star.

Anyway, Harry had been to see Johnny the day before and told me what to expect.

"He's a mess, Chey." Harry had come straight to my house after seeing him. "He hasn't showered; he's not even getting out of bed."

"What did he say about me?" I know how lame that sounds. I should've been asking about Johnny, but I was too far gone. My heart hurt so bad I thought it would burst.

"He's been pushing you away"—Harry paused for a second and then made air quotes—"for your own good."

"My own good?"

"He thinks you deserve to be with someone who isn't . . . who isn't . . ."

"Isn't what?"

Harry looked at the ground and said in a very soft voice, "deformed." Like I told you, Harry sees his scars as way worse than other people do. He kind of thinks he's the Elephant Man. I didn't know what to say.

Harry told me not to expect miracles. "I've been where Johnny is," he said. "He has a long, slow road to recovery, and there are going to be lots of ups and downs."

That phrase *lots of ups and downs* was echoing in my head when I rang Johnny's doorbell the next day. It was a Saturday, so I braced myself for his mother to answer. She hated me, thought I was a bad influence on her little angel. She loved to make little comments about how wrong I was for her son. "We're so proud Johnny got into Syracuse, aren't you? It will give him a chance to carve out a whole new life for himself, don't you think?" Only the last laugh was on her. Johnny's accident stopped him from ever going to Syracuse. I was ringing his doorbell in early August, and there he was—no way he would be leaving Yonkers.

I guess that sounds shitty. I don't mean it like that. I wish he had gotten to go to college. It's just that perfect little families are never perfect and sometimes when they get reminded of that, maybe it's not the worst thing in the world.

I guess that sounds shitty, too, so I should just shut up.

Anyway, I was ready for his mother. I was going to hold my tongue, grit my teeth, and smile. And if she didn't let me in to see him, I would just shove her out of the way.

Only, when the door opened it wasn't Mrs. McKenna, it was Johnny. He was showered, dressed in blue jeans and a Ramones T-shirt that he knew was my favorite, and he was standing with crutches. His right pant leg was tied up to just below his knee, but I hardly noticed that. It had been nearly a month since we'd been together and I was just so happy to see him.

I threw myself at Johnny and had him in a hug so fierce that I almost knocked him over.

"It's good to see you, too, Pick," he laughed.

Pick was the nickname Johnny gave me when I first joined the band. He only ever used it in private, one of our secrets. He loved that I played bass with a pick. I guess Dave, the bass player in the band before me, used his fingers. I never really got bass players who use their fingers. A pick makes such a badass sound, you know?

Anyway, Johnny and I went through his kitchen and down into the cathedral. It made me want to cry, watching him work his way down the stairs with his crutches and his missing leg.

Once we were sitting on the couch, he held my hand. The windows were open and there was a hot breeze; I was all clammy, but I think it was mostly from nerves.

"Why wouldn't you see me?" I was barking at him like one of the Dobermans from my neighborhood before he had a chance to say a word. He'd kept me away for so long that I'd convinced myself he hated me.

"It's tough to explain," he said, and he hung his head. Johnny's body language was all wrong. It was the first sign of how much everything had changed. "Harry really got on my case about it," he added.

"Harry? Got on *your* case?"

"I know, right? Him coming here was like a giant wake-up call, a giant alarm clock getting me out of bed."

I smiled, but all I could think was *Didn't you miss me?*

"We played music for hours. I didn't want it to end. It's the first time since this"—he motioned to his leg—"that I've really been happy."

"It's so good to see you, Johnny." I nuzzled my face into his neck, trying to turn the conversation back to us. Then I took his other hand, looked into his eyes, and kissed him. He seemed almost surprised. Not surprised that I kissed him, but surprised that he would be kissed at all, you know? But only for a minute. Then he kissed me back, and we were right where we left off.

Except . . . well, there was something different. I could feel it. It's like we were the same people, the same couple, but we were no longer *we*, if that makes sense. We were him and her, him and me.

Plus, there was something else. Something I needed to tell him. The other reason I was getting so desperate to see him.

I thought I was . . . well, I wasn't sure. Anyway, even if I had been sure, I couldn't lay that on Johnny. He was broken. I don't mean his leg; I mean Johnny the person. He was the most confident guy I'd ever known, and now he was broken. How could I tell him I thought I was pregnant?

PART TWO.
AUGUST TO OCTOBER 1986

*I put Catholic guilt to work pretty good
for a rich rock star.*
—Bono

Are you religious?

HARBINGER JONES

No.

I was a weird little kid, but I wasn't a bad little kid. I didn't torture animals, and I didn't set fires. I didn't wet the bed and I never tried to play doctor with any little girls. I didn't do anything to warrant the amount of abuse the universe has heaped on me. I refuse to believe this was the work of some sort of God, and if it was, well then, you know, fuck him.

CHEYENNE BELLE

You ever see the movie *Carrie*? My mom makes Carrie's mom look like an atheist.

I'm the oldest, and I was born before my parents were married. I think the guilt of having "conceived in sin" (my mom's words, not mine) is what drove her back to Mother Church. It's why I'm the only one of the Belle girls without a good Catholic name. I mean, think about it: Theresa, Agnes, Mary Elizabeth, Katherine, Patricia, Joan, and Cheyenne. One of these things does not belong with the others, right?

Anyway, I've been through Catholic school, CCD, and every kind of mass you can imagine. You can't turn a corner in my house without some image of Christ scaring the crap out of you. So am I religious? Yeah, but it's not like I had any choice.

RICHIE MCGILL

Yeah, I believe in God.

How else do you explain music?

CHEYENNE BELLE

It was about two weeks after I saw Johnny that I found out I was pregnant for sure. I was already pretty late with my period, though that isn't so strange for me (my cycle isn't anything you'd set your watch by). But it wasn't just that. I don't know how to describe it; I felt different.

I got one of those home pregnancy tests—actually, I got three of them (I would've bought more, but they're crazy expensive)—and the results were all the same: knocked up.

I was freaked out. And I was sick. A lot. I don't know why the hell they call it morning sickness when it comes at any time of the day. Do you know the only surefire cure for nausea? No? I'll tell you. Puking. You can drink all the ginger ale and eat all the saltine crackers you want. You wanna feel better? Woof your cookies.

Anyway, I couldn't tell any of the guys in the band I

was pregnant, so I talked to my younger sister Theresa. Or, really, she talked to me.

We were sitting on the beds in our room—Theresa and I shared a room with one of our other sisters, Agnes, but Agnes wasn't there—and I had my head leaned up against the wall, my hair matted against a movie poster of *Ladies and Gentleman, the Fabulous Stains*. It was really hot out, and I felt like I was going to be sick. Theresa took one look at me and knew.

"You're knocked up, aren't you?"

I'm guessing my jaw dropped. "Shit. You can tell?"

"You should go to Planned Parenthood."

"Planned Parenthood?"

"Yes. Get rid of it, Chey."

For some reason, I wasn't expecting her to say that, and it made me upset. Which made me feel more sick. I closed my eyes.

"Why?" I asked.

"Why get rid of it?" She sounded like she thought I was crazy for asking.

"Yeah. You tried to keep yours."

"And look what happened," she said. "God punished me."

Theresa had gotten pregnant two summers earlier, when she was fifteen, and lost her baby, at home, in bed. It was pretty messed up. She was, like, seven months, and the baby just started to come out. She tried to hide it, but with all that blood there was no hiding anything.

It had happened in the middle of the night, and somehow all of my sisters except for Agnes managed to sleep through it, even after the ambulance came. My parents, on the other hand, freaked out. My mother stood there in her bathrobe, clutching her rosaries and praying for the soul of the unborn baby. All I could think was *Shouldn't you be praying for Theresa?* My father kept mumbling something about killing "the boy who did this to my little girl."

The two of them went with Theresa to the hospital, but before they left my mother cornered me and Agnes: "Not one word of this to your sisters, do you understand?" She had fire and brimstone in her eyes.

"What are we supposed to tell them?"

"Tell them Theresa has the flu." Then she spun on her heel and climbed in the ambulance, still silently mouthing her prayers as she did. To this day I don't think any of my other sisters know.

I guess the conversation about me being pregnant was bringing back some pretty bad memories for Theresa, because she was squeezing the life out of Mr. Giggle Bunny. That's one of her stuffed animals.

My father's only emotional connection to his daughters has been to buy us stuffed animals. Lots and lots of stuffed animals. I have twelve and I'm a lightweight. There are one hundred twenty-six between all seven of us, and every one of them has been named. It's kind of a thing in our family.

"But won't God punish me more if I get rid of it?" I asked.

Most of the time I tried to be cool and scoff at all the Catholic stuff, but twelve years of religious education and a lifetime of being surrounded by religious paintings, statues, and lectures—well, you can take the girl out of the Church, but you can't take the Church out of the girl, you know? I started to cry.

Theresa rolled her eyes. "Just get it taken care of, Chey." It wasn't exactly mean, but it wasn't really helpful, either. She put her headphones back on, letting me know that the conversation was over. I guess, on some level, it felt good to get it off my chest, but really, talking to my sister was pretty much useless.

HARBINGER JONES

Once Johnny and I had reconnected, it was like an incredible weight had been lifted. Whatever Johnny's foibles and whatever my foibles, real friendships, I guess, run deep, and our friendship was real. But it wasn't perfect. Nothing ever is.

Even though Johnny wasn't mad at me anymore, I still felt responsible for him getting into the accident. I had driven him away from the band. I had pushed him to leave Georgia and go home to New York. And I was in love with his girlfriend. I may as well have held him down while that car rammed into his leg.

My shrink, Dr. Kenny, and I worked on the guilt, but I'm not sure it helped. The only thing that ever really seems to help me is playing music, so that's what I did.

CHEYENNE BELLE

Believe it or not, I went to confession.

I went to an all-girls Catholic high school where they force students to go to confession once a week. Most of the girls just made stuff up. "Forgive me, Father, for I had impure thoughts about this boy or that boy." Never "Forgive me, Father, for I went down on this boy *and* that boy," which was true a lot of the time.

Anyway, I hadn't been since I'd graduated a couple of months before, but I couldn't think of anywhere else to turn.

If you've never gone to confession, it's kind of weird. You sit in this dark little room that's like two phone booths smushed together; there's a wall dividing them down the middle and there's this little hole you talk into. The priest sits on the other side so he can't see you. I guess the idea is that he isn't supposed to know who's giving confession. But don't you think he peeks when people are coming and going? I know I would.

One time, in the tenth grade, I brought a flashlight with

me and shone it through the hole so I could get a good look at the priest. He didn't appreciate it.

They called my mom down to the school. She didn't appreciate it either.

Anyway, I told the priest a friend of mine was pregnant. (No way was I going to tell him the truth).

He said exactly what you'd expect a priest to say. "This is very serious. Has your friend told her parents?"

"No," I answered. "She doesn't have parents."

"Everyone has parents, my child." I never liked that, priests saying things like *my child*. I can't possibly be his child because he can't possibly have children, right? Though I suppose if I really believed that I wouldn't have been calling him Father, which I was.

"I mean, they're dead, Father."

"I see. Does she go to school here?"

"I'd rather not say."

"I understand that you want to protect your friend, but she needs help. She needs counseling."

I was quiet for a moment. I knew what I wanted to say but was having trouble working up the nerve. I have to give the man credit because he broke the silence with the question I needed to ask.

"Is this friend of yours considering having an abortion?"

"Yes, Father." I whispered my answer and wasn't even sure if he'd heard me.

"Abortion seems like an easy way out," he said, "but in life there are no easy ways out, my child."

I was surprised at how gentle he was being. I went in expecting him to shove a photo of a fetus or something through that little hole, but instead he was sort of comforting.

"But isn't she too young to have children?" I asked.

There was a long pause before he answered. I don't know if I was lucky or cursed to get the most thoughtful priest in the whole tristate area.

"Yes, yes, she is."

"Then shouldn't she end her pregnancy?"

"I think you know that abortion is a sin."

"Why?"

I could almost hear him wringing his hands. I felt sorry for the guy. He showed up at work expecting to hear the inane gossip of little girls and instead wound up with a real whopper of a problem dumped in his lap.

"It's murder."

"Do you really believe that?"

"I do."

"But I know girls who've had abortions, and they didn't burst into flames or anything. They seemed happier."

"A short-term reward in this life is no reward in the next." Priests were always saying stuff like that, and that's usually where they lost me.

"So my friend will go to hell, is that what you're saying?"

"This is not a sin that a few Hail Marys and Our Fathers will simply erase. It will haunt her for the rest of her days."

I don't remember the rest of the conversation, but I know I left pretty soon after his line about being haunted for the rest of my days. I was more confused than ever.

I tried to put it out of my mind, like a homework assignment I knew I was blowing off—I'm pretty good at keeping things in my life separate when I need to—and did the only thing I could think to do. I threw myself back into the band. Back into Johnny.

HARBINGER JONES

Because we were playing music again, all that other crap— my relationship with Johnny, my feelings for Chey—was pushed into the background, like hum, scratches, and static on a record. It's there, but soft enough that the music drowns it out. You still hear it between tracks, but only for a second.

Have you ever heard of something called signal-to-noise ratio? It's a term used by audiophiles. The wires that go from your turntable and your stereo to your speakers carry a signal that your speakers convert into sound. But the same wires are also loaded with extra noise generated by all those electrical components working at what they do. Your stereo and speakers filter most of it out. The more noise, the worse the signal and the worse the sound. Your goal in audio electronics is a lot of signal and very little noise.

The signal-to-noise ratio in my life at the end of that summer was really pretty good. The noise was still there, but having made peace with Johnny and having found a way to deal with my own feelings about Cheyenne, it was overwhelmed by signal.

Like I said, we were playing music again, and, really, that was all that mattered.

RICHIE MCGILL

I knew about the whole Harry, Johnny, Cheyenne love-triangle thing. I stayed away from that shit like it was the bubonic plague. I was just glad the band was back together. It was pretty much the only thing I had going for me.

I mean, skateboarding was fun, but it wasn't the same. The rush I get playing on stage is the reason I've never done drugs. From the first time Johnny got us together, way back in the seventh grade, and we played a few holiday parties, I was hooked. Playing music, when it works, is like sex. Just without all the mess. I knew nothing else could ever feel that good, so why bother?

CHEYENNE BELLE

I was able to keep the pregnancy a secret. Other than my nonexistent boobs, which had suddenly started to exist, I wasn't really showing. I got good at hiding the sickness, too, like I was bulimic or anorexic or something. It's kind of ironic that I was following in my sister's footsteps. Hiding a pregnancy, I mean.

Anyway, I thought about the baby all the time when I was alone. And I was so desperate to tell Johnny that I thought my head would explode. I just didn't know how.

I'd been teaching myself a little guitar—once you know how to play the bass, it's a lot easier to learn how to the play guitar—so I tried writing a song about it. I thought it would be cool to tell Johnny with a song. Sort of romantic, you know?

It was called "Lullaby."

> *Tell me,*
> *What's that in my belly*
> *Beneath the cat?*
> *I am making us a lullaby.*
>
> *Tell me,*
> *Can you feel this strange thing in my belly?*

Can you feel the change?
I'm too stunned to even cry.

Does it have a name?
Is it a boy or a girl?
Will it be president?
Will it change the world?
Will it be bad
Or will it be good?
Will it be loved
Or misunderstood?
Will it be rich
Or will it be poor?
Whatever it is,
I'm gonna love it forevermore.

Because you're our little lullaby.

There's more, but you get the idea.

I wanted so badly to play it for Johnny, but it just never felt like the right time, you know? So the secret stayed with me.

HARBINGER JONES

The other thing going on at the end of that summer was figuring out how to keep my parents at bay. To be fair, they were giving me space, but I knew it wouldn't last, especially with my dad.

I was already back on Dr. Kenny's couch at my parents' insistence—Dr. Kenny had been my shrink ever since I was eight years old, since right after the lightning strike—and it was only a matter of time before they started to push on other things, too. I mean, I was eighteen, I wasn't enrolled in college, and I didn't have a job. Johnny's accident and my reaction to it bought me a little time, but sooner or later they were going to expect something more of me than eating their food, lying on their couch, watching their TV, and using their basement to play music.

But like everything else in my life, I kicked the can down the road. I figured I'd ride it as long as I could.

CHEYENNE BELLE

This was all happening at the same time the band started jamming again.

"Harry," Johnny said at one of our first rehearsals after Georgia, "you should be singing some of our songs."

"What? No."

I had told Johnny about Harry's incredible night as our front man at the keg party in Athens.

"Seriously, dude, we're called the Scar Boys, not the Amputee Boys. You and I should share the mic. You sing some of the songs, I'll sing some of the songs."

Harry fought it at first, but in the end he agreed. I could tell it made him really happy, too.

I honestly think Johnny figured getting Harry, our original "scar boy," up front would help the band. But there was something else, too. Johnny was tired. Really tired. He was going to rehab four times a week, and it was taking a toll.

He let me come with him once and I was surprised at how simple it was. I expected to see medieval torture devices clipped to his leg while he learned how to walk. Instead, it was just a plastic leg with a foam foot that he would practice walking on for about an hour. The leg, Johnny said, was temporary.

"They don't give you your permanent leg until you're fully healed," he told me. "They have to wait until the stump is done morphing and changing shape before they can create a mold to fit the prosthesis."

It's weird how comfortable I got with words like *stump* and *prosthesis*. It's like they'd always been part of my vocabulary, part of my life.

Johnny had been lucky . . . well, as lucky as you can be when you have your leg chopped off. The break was clean, and his skin was intact. Apparently, what happens to your skin when you lose a limb is really important. Johnny didn't need any skin grafts, which was good. Plus, because of the way the break happened, the surgery was pretty straightforward. It was really easy for them to fit him for a new leg.

Even in the worst of times, the best things still happened to Johnny McKenna.

The day I went with him to rehab, I saw all sorts of other amputees in much worse shape than Johnny. There was one girl with a leg that was so badly scarred that I wondered what kind of accident she'd been in. It made me think of Harry.

Johnny's recovery seemed easier than I would've guessed. He was a fast learner, and after six weeks his rehab went from four to two times a week, and after three months he was pretty much done. You could barely tell he had a limp.

He'd been all set to go to Syracuse on a track-and-field scholarship before the accident, and it was really important to him to learn how to run with his new leg. Johnny probably had some secret dream that he'd be the first amputee to win a track-and-field medal at the Olympics, and I don't mean the Special Olympics.

Anyway, even though the rehab was going really well, it was still a strain for him to spend a lot of time on his fake leg. His stump would get blisters if he put pressure on it for too long, so standing in front of a microphone for two hours during rehearsals wasn't really in the cards. He never actually told me that, but I could tell.

Since he couldn't stand, do you know what Johnny did instead?

Johnny McKenna decided to play the piano.

HARBINGER JONES

Johnny confided in me that standing up for two hours—that's how long our rehearsals usually lasted—was too much for his leg.

"Imagine leaning your elbow on a table for two hours," he told me. "Even if that elbow is on a nice soft cushion, the weight of your body will eventually wear it down. It's like that." The keyboard gave him a chance to sit. It, along with piano lessons, had been a present from his parents. Really, it was a kind of bribe to get him to reengage with the world.

I'd seen that kind of thing before. My parents showered me with gifts after the lightning strike. I was only eight when I spent all that time in the hospital, and I got an endless assortment of books and games and toys. I didn't get anything as cool as an electric keyboard, though. I mean, the greatest thing about 1976 was the Pet Rock. Enough said.

When we started jamming again with the whole band,

Johnny refused to plug the keyboard in, so he would just play along silently. He was something of a perfectionist. Strike that. He didn't need things to be perfect; he needed them to be as good as they could be. There's a difference.

But he did plug the piano in when it was just the two of us. That gave him a chance to fool around and learn how to make the keys work with another instrument. Hearing the keyboard and guitar together was like discovering an entire new universe. Like our own, it was filled with planets and stars and people. But in this universe, the laws of physics were expanded to allow for new dimensions. It was unreal.

CHEYENNE BELLE

For most of those first two months of the band jamming again, in August and September, Johnny sat behind his keyboard, trying to find the right notes. We didn't know if he was any good or not because he wouldn't plug the damn thing in.

"Not until I get better at this," he would say.

We all just took it in stride. It didn't matter. He sat on his stool and sang the songs that Harry didn't want to sing, and it was like it was in the early days of the band. We just practiced and had fun hanging out together.

But there were undercurrents. There are always undercurrents. No matter what you're doing in life, there is always something written between the lines. Nothing is ever exactly what it seems.

Take my father.

No, I mean, please, take my father. Ha ha. I'm mostly kidding. I love my dad, but he doesn't really have much on the ball. Harry calls him the La-Z-Man because he never leaves his La-Z-Boy. There's a reason the chair manufacturer named it that. My dad just sits there in front of the TV, zoning out.

He's retired on disability. I'm not even sure what that really means. I just know he gets a check every month for not working. So I guess that's a kind of work. In some weird way, it's like he's getting paid for watching TV all day. And for drinking.

And no, we don't need to go there. I know my dad is a drunk. My sisters know my dad is a drunk. The neighbors know my dad is a drunk. My friends know my dad is a drunk. The only two people in the entire city who don't seem to know that my dad is a drunk are my dad and my mom.

Anyway, my dad just sort of gave up on life. He and my mom had all these daughters, and I think he got overwhelmed and packed it in. But here's the thing: sometimes, when he's watching television, his attention wanders. His eyes focus on a spot above and behind the TV, like he sees something there. I wonder if he's seeing his life without the rest of us, without me, my mom, and my sisters. Or maybe he's seeing what his life would have been like if the rest of us hadn't come along in the first place.

Undercurrents.

There were undercurrents at our rehearsals, too. At first I thought it was just my pregnancy freaking me out, but after a while I realized it was other stuff, too.

Mostly, it was Johnny and Harry. Johnny, because he was trying to figure out how to live life without his leg—I don't mean physically, I mean emotionally—and Harry, because had a pretty big crush on me.

Harry said the crush was over. He told me he was happy that we could be friends and happy that the band was back together. But I saw the way he still looked at me. Not like he was undressing me with his eyes or anything pervy, more like he was trying to hold my hand with his eyes. Most days, it broke my heart. Not a lot, just a little. What's that expression? Death by a thousand cuts? Like that.

Harry had figured out how to tuck his feelings away so they weren't causing any problems in the band, but the crush was still there, underneath the surface, like a bruise under your skin. I know that must sound conceited, but it's the truth.

Like, one time, I was walking by and gave Harry a

little squeeze on the neck, and I felt his whole body go stiff. Anytime I'd done that in the past, he would sort of just melt into me, like a puppy. But now, now things were different.

"You okay?" I asked him.

"Yeah, yeah, I'm fine." We locked eyes for a minute, and I thought he was going to cry. He wasn't fine. I knew from that moment on that Harry was off-limits.

All that stuff was in the background, but it was there. There was a lot of baggage, and there were a lot of secrets.

Anyway, we played and played, day after day, grinding out song after song in Harry's basement. None of us had jobs, and other than Richie going to school every day—he was still a senior in high school—and Johnny going to physical therapy, we focused on the band. It was an endless stream of rehearsals, each one the same as the one before. Even my morning sickness had settled down into something I could manage.

Sooner or later, something had to change. I figured it would be my pregnancy—that was like a bomb with a timer counting down to zero—but Richie pushed a different button first.

"So you ever gonna plug that fucking thing in or what?" he said to Johnny at the end of one rehearsal.

Johnny did, and the Scar Boys were *truly* reborn.

RICHIE MCGILL

What did I think when Johnny started playing the piano? Shit, I didn't think about it at all. I just let the groove into my bones, and, man, it felt good.

CHEYENNE BELLE

Before Johnny sat down at the piano, we were guitar, bass, drums, and vocals, like the Who or R.E.M. And we were good. We were really good.

The bass and drums together, the way Richie and I played them, were like a grandfather clock or a heartbeat. They provided a road map for the guitar and vocal. Or maybe they were like a trail map, because more often than not Johnny and Harry would wander off the trail, always finding their way back out of the woods. It was beautiful.

But the piano was something else. Most people think a piano is a string instrument. I mean, it makes sense. Vibrating strings make the notes, right? But it's not. Little hammers hit those strings to make them vibrate, so a piano is a *percussion* instrument. Did you know that? Don't feel bad; most people don't. The point is, a piano is like the bass, drums, and guitar, all together. It's a whole band inside one box. So when you add a guitar, bass, and drums on top of a piano, it's . . . it's . . . exponential.

Johnny's private lessons and hours and hours of practice had paid off. Like everything else in his life, being good at playing keyboards just came naturally to him. He added rhythm to the songs we already knew and brought new songs to the band based on some piano riff he'd whipped up. The riffs were always incredibly simple—even Johnny wasn't going to turn into Billy Joel after just a couple of months—but they always worked.

We were all blown away. Well, Richie and I were blown away. It seemed like Harry already knew.

The first new song Johnny brought to the band, the same day he finally plugged in his keyboard, was called "That's Not My Leg." It had an Allman Brothers, chunky groove of mostly G and C chords, and he played the piano more like bongos than anything else, beating on it with his hands, keeping time like a drummer.

As soon as Johnny started to play, Harry added the perfect guitar riff, like he'd heard the song before. I couldn't be sure at first because Harry was like that. He's a guitar genius, always playing exactly the right thing at exactly the right time. But any doubt I had went away when they started singing the song together.

Hey, Doctor, put away your saw.
I don't want to see my leg lying on

your operating room floor.
Don't tell me to count backward from ten.
I don't want to go to sleep and never
see my leg again.

(Harry) Ten.
Take this mask off my face.
(Harry) Nine.
Get me out of this place.
(Harry) Eight.
I've got to hold on.
(Harry) Seven.
Oh, no, I'm gone.

That's not my leg
Below my knee.
That's not my leg
Strapped to me.
Doctor!
That's not my leg.

"Fucking A!" Richie was right. It was really, really good. But I couldn't get over the fact that they'd written it, had figured it all out, without me. Not only that, but Johnny, who wouldn't plug that piano in for anyone, had been playing it for Harry.

I know, I was crazy to be jealous of them. Everything in the world was better when Johnny and Harry were getting along. But I couldn't help feeling like I was on the outside looking in.

"Dudes," Richie said, "play that again." And they did. And we did. Richie and I added the backbone, and the first new Scar Boys song in more three months was brought into the world.

"We need to play out," Richie said.

Harry and Johnny looked at each other, then back at the two of us, and said together: "CBGB's."

HARBINGER JONES

This is going to sound counterintuitive, but my favorite place in the world is to be onstage. Part of it is that the guitar and the music act like a shield, protecting me from everything bad. But another part is that I get to step out of my skin and become someone else. Wait, strike that. I get to step out of this costume that's been forced on me and become who I'm really supposed to be. For a little while, I'm not this damaged little turd; I'm a rock star.

I know I'm not actually a rock star, but it's how I feel, and that's what's important.

That we now had a date on the calendar for a gig in what was basically our homeport, was like a tonic for me. I was so excited I could barely contain myself.

I couldn't freaking wait.

CHEYENNE BELLE

I was maybe twelve weeks pregnant when Johnny called CBGB's and about sixteen weeks when we actually played the gig.

The last time we'd played CBGB's was in May, and this was the end of October. We'd started to gain a bit of a following before we left on our tour, so it was easy enough to get a gig. Carol, the booking agent, put us right back onto a Thursday night, a prime spot. She gave us a slot opening for a band from out of town called Chemicals Made of Mud. Mud, as we called them, was touring the US in support of a record they had just put out on Twin/Tone. That was the label that put out the Replacements and Soul Asylum and was something of a Holy Grail to indie bands, so we were ready to be impressed.

We weren't.

Not only were the guys in Mud jerks—the guitar player hit on me all night long—their music sucked. It was like art-house rock meets the Osmond family. I think they were going for kitsch. That doesn't work. Something is kitsch or it's not. Like *Rocky Horror*. When they were making that movie, I don't think they knew how campy and ridiculous it was. Or maybe they did and they didn't care. They were just having fun. Mud, on the other hand, was trying too hard, and it wasn't working.

Before they played, it was our job to "warm up" the crowd. That's such a stupid phrase. People in nightclubs are plenty warm to begin with, you know?

I was surprised that, when we took the stage, we actually had fans there. I thought being away for so long would've been death for the Scar Boys, that we would've needed to start all over again, but it wasn't and we didn't.

We opened with a couple of our standards—"Girl in the Band" and "Girl Next Door." Every note of those two songs was exactly what we wanted it to be but better, mostly because the piano made everything sound entirely new.

Just like the last time we were at CB's, the crowd grabbed on to our music. The small group of fans that started the set with us, the dozen or so kids who were cheering when we took the stage, were slowly joined by the rest of the audience—mostly Mud fans, I guess—so that by the middle of our set, the whole place was jumping.

We closed with "Like Us," our usual closing number, and we got called back for an encore.

We played "That's Not My Leg," with Johnny singing lead.

Just as we were grooving up to the last bar of the final chorus, Johnny took the mic out of its stand and hobbled out from behind the keyboard. In order to play up the name of the band, Johnny wasn't wearing his prosthetic leg. Instead, he had on a peg leg, like a pirate's peg leg.

"Where the hell did you get that thing?" Richie had asked as Johnny strapped it on before the gig.

"Secondhand shop."

"You can buy peg legs at secondhand shops?" I asked.

"Trust me," he said, smiling. "This is going to help us tonight."

I looked at the other guys. Richie just shrugged. Harry had his head down, his hat pulled low. Something was up, but I had no idea what.

Anyway, like I was saying, Johnny and his peg leg came out from behind the keyboard during our encore of "That's Not My Leg." Right when Johnny was getting up, Harry strummed one loud chord and let the sustain mix with the feedback from his amp. It created a sound like a distorted, pissed-off Liberty Bell. As it rang, he lifted his guitar strap over his head and held the guitar by the body, shaking it so the ringing started to oscillate. Johnny, still singing, moved to the middle of the stage and locked eyes with Harry. I had no idea what they were up to, so I kept playing the bass. I glanced back at Richie, but he was too wrapped up in what was going on in front of us to notice me. He kept the frantic beat chugging, and I kept up with him.

Just as we were getting close to the last note of the song, Harry crouched down low. I didn't understand what was happening, so I wasn't ready when he swung his guitar at Johnny's peg leg. Johnny leaped into the air the instant the guitar struck wood, and the leg went sailing into the crowd. Johnny stuck the landing on his one good foot, both arms held high over his head like a gymnast. I shrieked but somehow managed to keep it together long enough to end the song on time with Richie.

The audience went batshit crazy. It's what it must've been like to see Pete Townshend smash his first guitar.

HARBINGER JONES

"I'm sorry, you want me to do what?" I asked.

We were in the cathedral, Johnny's living room.

"Just try it. I promise, it won't hurt me." Johnny could barely contain his excitement. I hadn't seen him this animated since his accident. He'd been coming around slowly, but this was a new level of engagement.

"Let me get this straight," I said, trying to make sure I understood what he was asking. "You want me to swing my guitar at your prosthetic leg, and swing it hard enough to knock it over."

"Yes."

"John, I don't think I can do that."

"Of course you can."

"Okay, let's come at this from a different angle. Why would I want to do that?"

"Because I wrote a new song, and it's the best way— it's the only way—to end it."

That's when Johnny played "That's Not My Leg" for the first time. Of course, I loved it from the second I heard it. It was the perfect anthem for a band of disfigured, disabled kids called the Scar Boys.

Now I understood what he was asking. I still didn't like it, but I understood it.

"Let's practice it a few times without the music," he said. "Just to see how it goes."

"Isn't that thing strapped to you somehow? Won't it break the straps?" I paused as I thought about it. "And, hey, wait, won't it break my guitar?"

I'm not proud that I cared more about the guitar than I cared about Johnny's leg, but, you know, it was my guitar.

"I haven't fully figured out the straps thing yet, so for now I'll leave it loose. My stump will just be resting on it. If we time it right, if I jump at just the right instant, the guitar should sail through the leg, no problem."

"No problem," I muttered under my breath. But I nodded my assent.

Johnny was smiling like a deranged lunatic as he stood up and made his way out from behind the keyboard into the middle of the room. He took a minute to pull down the neoprene sleeve wrapped around his leg, making sure it was loose. When he was done, he was leaning on it the way someone with two legs might lean their knee on a coffee table.

"Okay, you're sure about this?"

"Just do it already!"

So I lifted the guitar strap over my head and held my Strat by its neck, like a baseball bat. I crouched low, readying myself to swing.

When I was younger, before I knew Johnny, before I played the guitar, I took a few Tae Kwon Do lessons. My dad thought it was a way I could build confidence. One of the first things they taught me was how to break a board. I'm not kidding; just to get your white belt you actually had to break a piece of wood with your hand. I can still remember standing in the class.

"My name is Harry, and my breaking board is hammer fist, sir!" I yelled. Then I cocked my arm high over my head and brought it down gently once, touching the board and saying, "Concentration." I recocked the arm and brought it down gently again, this time saying, "Confidence." The third time, I brought the arm down with all the force my ten-year-old body could muster, screaming, *"Ki hap!"* It was a kind of Korean power word. No one was more surprised than me when my hand sliced through that board like it was a piece of paper.

It was an incredibly happy moment—one of the happiest of my life—for about ten seconds. That's when one of the other students in the class said, "It looks like someone did breaking board on his face," and all the other kids laughed.

The teacher, who I really admired, admonished the other kids, talking to them about respect, but I could still see the look in their eyes. I was going to be the freak in Tae Kwon Do just like I was in school, and I didn't want that.

I never went back.

I wish I had, though. I really wish I had.

That day in Johnny's living room, I brought the guitar back, gently moved it forward to the prosthetic leg, and said, "Concentration." I brought it back and moved it forward again, saying the second part of my incantation: "Confidence." But when I swung through the third time, the moment of the lethal strike, I pulled up, holding back any real power. I hit Johnny's leg with all the force of a down pillow. The leg wobbled like a bowling pin but didn't fall over.

Johnny groaned. "Jesus Christ, Harry. You have to hit it. Are you scared or something?" It was a dickish kind of thing for him to say, but in a way it made me happy; it was a sign that the old Johnny was trying to fight his way back into the world.

"Okay, okay, let's try again." This time my third blow was what it needed to be, and his leg went flying across the room, landing on a sofa. Johnny had jumped in the air at just the right instant and managed to land on his good leg, though he had to hold on to a table to keep from losing his balance and falling over.

"Yes!" Johnny was totally pumped at how well the stunt had worked. "That's it! Let's do it again!"

I retrieved Johnny's leg, and we set up to run through it once more. Just as my guitar was sailing through the air and connecting with Johnny's prosthesis, Mrs. McKenna, Johnny's mom, turned a corner on the top of the stairs. She shrieked as she watched the leg go flying through the air, this time knocking over a lamp.

"Are you boys insane!"

She spent the next ten minutes screaming at us about the cost of a prosthetic leg, not to mention the lamp, not to mention the damage we could do to Johnny. We were very apologetic and very contrite. She ended with an "I think you'd better go now, Harry."

Johnny walked me out. When we got to my car, he smiled and said, "Okay, we'll need to practice that one at your house." And that's just what we did.

When we finally got around to doing it at the gig, it

came off—the stunt and the leg—without a hitch. Johnny, realizing his mother was right about needing to protect his prosthesis, somehow managed to get his hands on a peg leg. When that gnarled piece of wood went sailing through the air, it was like the Bat-Signal letting all of Gotham City know that the Scar Boys were back.

I was a little surprised at how pissed off Cheyenne was when we got to the greenroom, and it made me feel a little bad, but honestly, at that point, she was Johnny's problem, not mine.

CHEYENNE BELLE

"What the fuck was that?!" I screamed at Harry and Johnny the second we got to the graffiti-covered excuse for a dressing room behind the stage. I know the other guys see the romance of CBGB's, but to me that place is a dump.

"C'mon, what?" Johnny answered, laughing. "Did you see how much they liked it?" He was sitting on the bench, pulling on the custom-made sock that sat in the socket of his real prosthetic leg.

"Yeah, well, maybe you two idiots could've warned me first." Harry was trying hard to stifle a laugh. Johnny wasn't even trying; he was doubled over, the jerk.

"I didn't know, either," Richie offered, all serious. Then he burst out laughing too, adding, "But it was fucking awesome! How many times did you guys practice that?"

I was pissed off and I was hurt, so I left the dressing room and went out front while Mud played their set.

Like I said, they weren't much to watch. The five members of the band—two guitars, bass, drums, vocal—all had Beatlesque haircuts, flannel shirts, jeans, and ratty sneakers. It was a uniform for alt rockers that had already become a cliché. They pranced around the stage like it was some weird kind of ballet. I was embarrassed for them.

They were playing a song called "I'm Sick and Tired of Being Sick and Tired." The lead singer, so pleased with how clever the lyric was, could barely contain his smirk as he sang that line over and over again. And the guitar player, who moved like he was double-jointed—by that, I mean like a real spaz—kept winking at me. Actually winking. I mean, who does that?

Anyway, right at that exact moment, the entire world stopped spinning.

Or maybe my brain sped up, I don't know.

Each beat of the snare echoed and boomed for an eternity.

Every wink of that creepy guitar player's eyelid was like a curtain slowly coming down.

Every word that singer sang was a drawn-out slur.

Time did everything it could to stop.

Sitting at that crusty, crappy table in the cesspit that is CBGB's, on the heels of a great Scar Boys set, after Johnny and Harry had played their trick that had so pissed me off, in the middle of the ridiculousness of "I'm Sick and Tired of Being Sick and Tired" by Chemicals Made of Mud, the dumbest band in the history of dumb bands, I felt the baby move for the first time.

Holy shit, the baby—my baby—was moving.

I knew without any trace of doubt I was going to keep it.

PART THREE,
NOVEMBER 1986

A ballad once in a while doesn't go amiss.
—Chrissie Hynde

Who are your musical influences?

HARBINGER JONES

The Bay City Rollers.

CHEYENNE BELLE

The Bay City Rollers.

RICHIE MCGILL

Let me guess, the other guys said the Bay City Rollers?

Yeah, we all hate that question. It's, like, the most unoriginal question in the universe, and we swore that if anyone ever asked it, we would all always say the Bay City Rollers.

But I kind of like you, so I'm gonna give you a break and give you my real answer.

You ready?

The Bay City Rollers.

HARBINGER JONES

We decided to take the next day off from rehearsal.

But I never take a day off from the guitar. I was hanging out in the basement in my parents' house, watching *The Price is Right*, the guitar on my lap.

After a while I found myself picking the same riff over and over again. It was kind of beautiful. Maybe that sounds immodest, but it's the only word I can use to describe what I was hearing. Everything around me dropped away. The TV became a blur of muted color, the cheering of the game-show audience faded to static. The only thing I could hear was that riff.

That's kind of amazing because my guitar wasn't even plugged in. When you play the electric guitar, you can barely hear it if it's not plugged in. But when you play often enough, your brain interprets what little sound there is and compensates for it. It's like my brain engaged some sort of organic alpha-wave amplifier that allowed me to hear that riff with perfect clarity.

I played it over and over again until it had the rhythm and cadence of a slow-moving train. Next thing I knew, my hands shifted to a chord progression built off the line I'd been playing, and I knew I had a song.

I started singing, the words more or less coming to me without interruption.

I bet when authors write books, they probably get

into a zone where whole chapters pour out of them without ever once needing Wite-Out. That's what happened to me.

A song. This song. It was just floating in the air or in my brain, or maybe in the background hum of Bob Barker hawking everyday household items, and somehow it came out of my hands and out of my mouth. It was a kind of magic.

When I was done, I turned the TV off and called Johnny. Someone needed to hear this.

"Yeah," Johnny said when I called him. "C'mon over, I'm just listening to music."

I could hear in his voice that Johnny was kind of out of it. He had good days and bad days, and after the excitement of the CB's gig, I think he was having a bad day. I didn't really like to be around Johnny when he was like that—I guess I saw too much of myself in him; it hit too close to home—but I also knew that's when he needed me the most.

He was sitting on the floor of his bedroom when I got to his house, his back leaning up against his desk. Above his head, on the desk blotter, were three brown vials of prescription medicines. I couldn't read the labels, but figured they must be painkillers or antibiotics to stave off any infection that might have lingered in his stump. I used to have those little bottles lined up in my room, too.

A coiled wire snaked down from a hi-fi unit to a pair of headphones wrapped around Johnny's ears. His eyes were closed, and he was otherwise motionless. The album cover for U2's *Wide Awake in America* was on the floor.

The record is an EP, just four songs. "Bad," an eight-minute live opus that pulls you through every emotion you can imagine, was a favorite song of ours. Both Johnny and I felt like Bono was talking to us personally.

I nudged Johnny's foot with the toe of my sneaker.

"Careful, Harry," he said without opening his eyes. "I've only got one of those left."

"I know it's the left, and that ain't right," I answered. This had quickly become a favorite joke of ours. I don't know why. "'Bad'?" I asked about the music.

"Actually, pretty damn good." Johnny and I were a regular Smothers Brothers. No, strike that. More like Martin and Lewis. We were still a bit too dysfunctional to be the Smothers Brothers.

"So let's hear this new song," he said, tugging the headphones down around his neck.

I was about to take my Strat out of its case, but I realized this would sound much better on an acoustic guitar. Music is like that. You need the right tools to make it perfect. So I grabbed Johnny's Takamine. It had a sunburst body with a built-in pickup and this trebly sound with a lot of twang. It was bright and clear, like sunshine.

I sat on Johnny's bed and started picking, and right away I saw him smiling. He recognized the guitar part for what it was: a really good riff. I was just about to launch into the lyrics and melody when my brain hit the pause button. *Oh, shit,* I thought. *I can't sing this song for Johnny.*

CHEYENNE BELLE

After feeling the baby move, I knew I couldn't put it off anymore, so I got up super early the day after the gig, like eight thirty, took the number twenty bus up Central Avenue, got off at Underhill, and walked the rest of the way to Johnny's house. The walk is way more than a mile, first up and then down a steep hill. I was tired and not feeling quite right, and by the time I got there, almost two hours after I left home, I was a bit of a wreck.

"Do you want me to come with you?" Theresa had asked from her bed as I was leaving the house. She was still bleary from whatever she'd been doing the night before. Part of me really wanted to have someone with me when I told Johnny, but I knew I needed to do this alone. I told her, "No, thanks." She nodded, flopped her head back down on the pillow, and was snoring before I left the room.

I didn't even know if Johnny was home, which, given how I was feeling, I suppose was pretty stupid. I don't know why I didn't call first. Maybe I wanted to catch him off guard, or maybe I wanted to see how happy he would be when I showed up at his door. Or maybe I just wasn't thinking straight.

When I got there my heart sank to my knees; Harry's car was in the driveway. I felt like I couldn't catch a break.

Yeah, I should've been happy that Johnny and Harry were back to the way they were when I first joined the band. They'd been rebuilding their broken friendship brick by brick since we got back from Athens, and by this time it was stronger than ever. I guess it had to do with Johnny's accident. Misery really does love company, you know? If I'm being honest, I wonder if my decision to keep the baby was me wanting to find a way to be closer to Johnny than Harry was.

God, it sounds so messed up to say that out loud.

Anyway, Johnny answered the door, and he *was* happy to see me. Even though he was on crutches without his prosthetic leg, he wrapped me in a big hug and didn't let go for a long minute. That goofy "I Melt with You" song popped into my head.

"C'mon in, Pick. Harry's here. We're working on a new song. You should hear it."

Harry stood up when we walked into Johnny's bedroom. He always did that when I came into a room. Always a little too quickly, always with his shoulders and neck a little too stiff.

"Oh, hey, Chey," he said to me, and then turned to Johnny. "I can get going. We can finish this later."

"No, stay, stay. Play the song for Chey." Johnny eased himself onto the folding chair behind his keyboard. We were cramped in there, and I felt like the walls were closing in. Harry looked at me, waiting for some cue, some hint to know whether he should stay or go. I needed to tell Johnny my news—our news—and I wanted Harry out of there in the worst possible way, but I was kind of stuck. I didn't know how to ask him to leave without giving everything away.

Anyway, maybe Harry could read all that in my eyes, because he said, "No, really, I should go. I'll play it for the whole band when we jam Monday."

"Stop," Johnny said. "Just play it. Really, she's going to love it."

Classic Johnny. Issuing orders and talking about other people like they weren't in the room. As much as all of our relationships had grown and changed, the foundation of who we were was the same. While it didn't happen as much as it used to, when Johnny gave a command Harry was programmed to follow.

Harry sat down on the edge of the bed, lifted Johnny's acoustic onto his lap, and started picking. I leaned against the doorjamb, listening and watching.

Harry was nervous. I could tell because he does this

thing with his forehead, crinkling the place where his eyebrows should be, kind of like a pug. The music was much slower and more ballady than anything we'd ever played before. But the riff was hypnotic. It was haunting. Then Harry began to sing.

> *Phones ring.*
> *Voices meander, like waves*
> *beating up the air.*
> *None of those voices ever sing.*
> *She wonders if*
> *She even cares.*
>
> *She's nearly a saint.*
> *And no one notices when*
> *she scrapes the ground.*
> *She wishes she had the time*
> *To hear pleasant sounds.*

He stopped.

"I'm still working on some of the lyrics, but it has a bridge, too." He started strumming, going from the main riff to a series of power chords.

Run away,

Go away,

Hide away,

Sneak away.

There's got to be an easier way

To face each day.

Then the bridge flowed back to the main riff, like a musical river.

Her ears ring,

Deafened by noise of boys playing with toys.

But the noise is nothing;

Maybe it's why she's so silently annoyed.

Johnny started messing around on the piano, but I wished he hadn't. It almost ruined the moment.

"Pleasant Sounds"—that's what it's called—was maybe the most beautiful song I'd ever heard. And here's the thing: I knew it was about me.

I could see it in Harry's eyes.

I could feel it in the chords.

I can't really explain it. I just somehow knew.

Johnny was clueless. When it came to music, he wasn't the same as the rest of us. Johnny was, in some ways, the most talented guy in the band, but it was coming from a different place. With me and Richie and Harry, it came from the heart. With Johnny, it came from the head. I actually think that's a good thing for a band, to have some of it coming from the heart and some of it coming from the head.

Anyway, Harry and I were in the middle of sharing this incredible moment, and Johnny was sitting there, grinning like an idiot, missing the whole thing.

"Isn't that great?" he said to me. "Don't you love it?" he pushed. Johnny always pushed.

I started to cry. Maybe it was the pregnancy hormones, or maybe the song was just that beautiful, or maybe the long walk from the number twenty bus had done me in. Whatever the reason, I lost it.

"Chey?" Johnny asked, this time with a gentle voice.

"I'll leave you guys alone," Harry said. He put down the acoustic guitar, picked up his Strat, and walked out of the room. I heard the front door to Johnny's house close, and we were alone.

"Pick, are you okay?" Johnny pulled himself up—like I said, he wasn't wearing his leg—and took a hopping step toward me. I saw him stifle a grimace of pain as he tried to pull me into an embrace. It didn't work.

We flopped down together on the bed, Johnny landing on top of me, pretty hard.

I panicked for a second, thinking, like, *Oh, crap, did he just squash the baby?* But even I knew that was silly. He must've seen my eyes go wide or heard me gasp with fear or something.

"Chey, I'm sorry. . . . I'm not . . . it's not what you think."

It would've been so easy to just tell him right then and there. To say, "No, Johnny, I don't think you're hitting on me. It's that I'm worried about the baby in my belly. Our baby." But I couldn't. His eyes were darting back and forth, and they were all glassy. Everything about him seemed lost, like he was in some kind of maze and couldn't find his way out. Johnny was still going through so much shit that I couldn't dump this gigantic thing on him. I just couldn't. It would just have to wait a few more days.

I managed to choke back my tears and tried to smile.

"No, it's okay," I whispered, talking about us falling onto the bed. "I know, I know."

And then Johnny McKenna did something I'd never seen him do before.

He started crying.

HARBINGER JONES

It got way more complicated when Chey showed up. I mean, the song was about her. Of course it was about her.

I didn't realize that when I was writing it. Sometimes the words and music just pour out and you have no idea what they mean until much later.

In the case of "Pleasant Sounds," I understood the meaning as soon as I started playing the guitar riff for Johnny. But once I'd started picking the notes, I was trapped.

I kind of hiccupped when I sang the first line—*Phones ring*—my voice catching like it was tripping over the edge of a carpet. And I mumbled. But it didn't matter.

Johnny, who is smarter than me most of the time, is kind of dumb in a couple of very specific ways. It would never occur to him that I would write a song about Cheyenne. Whether that's because he and I are best friends and he and Chey are together, or whether it's because he thinks someone like me has no business fantasizing about someone like Cheyenne, I have no idea.

So I finished the song, and Johnny was just beaming. I could tell that he really loved it, and that put me at ease.

"We have to add this to our set right away. Play it again."

So I did, and he started messing around with some piano parts.

Then the doorbell rang.

In the two minutes Johnny was gone answering the door, my nerves started jangling. I was pretty sure it was Chey. It's like the universe suddenly notices that I'm doing kind of okay and then it rings the doorbell to set things straight.

When Chey walked into the room trailing Johnny, I felt an overwhelming need to get the hell out of there. I tried, but Johnny kind of forced me to play the song.

Again, I was trapped.

I know what you're thinking. *How can he force you, Harry?*

There was too much history between Johnny and me for it to work any other way. It's hard to explain.

I played the song with my eyes shut the entire time. When I finished, Cheyenne just started bawling. She knew right away that the song was about her. Johnny looked confused.

I grabbed my guitar and left, feeling pretty shell-shocked. I figured Chey was crying over the guilt of her and me having kissed in Georgia and that she was going to tell Johnny everything.

Yes, we kissed. It was one time, it lasted all of five seconds, and it never happened again. It was right after Johnny had quit the tour and gone home, and we were all a bit confused. In the end, it didn't mean anything. But I knew Johnny wouldn't see it that way. He would see it as a betrayal, and I couldn't blame him.

I sat in my car, waiting for them to come storming out of the house. I had this mental image of Johnny hopping over to my window and bludgeoning me with his prosthetic leg. When that didn't happen, I thought about going back inside and confronting them, but who was I kidding? There was no way that was going to happen.

All the good stuff in my life that had started to take root was about to be wiped away, again. It was like getting your favorite cassette tape too close to a magnet, all your favorite tracks jumbled and gone.

I started on one of my lists. It's a trick Dr. Kenny taught me when I was a kid. I memorize and recite boring lists of things; it's supposed to help calm me down. Anything from naming all the presidents or Oscar winners to memorizing recipe ingredients or children's books, whatever will force my mind in a different direction.

It works every time.

I was up to the forty-ninth digit of pi—five, in case you're wondering—and it was starting to have an effect. I was settling down, and I knew it was time to leave.

I had my hand on the gearshift, getting ready to back out of Johnny's driveway, when Chey stepped out of the front door. She had stopped crying, but she looked bewildered and more than a little bit freaked out.

"You want a ride?" I asked through the open window.

She didn't say anything or even look at me as she opened the door and took a seat. Not knowing what else to do, I pulled out of the driveway and rolled on down the hill.

We cruised streets in Yonkers, Tuckahoe, and Eastchester for at least ten minutes in total silence. At first I was nervous as hell. I was pretty sure that whatever had happened between Johnny and Cheyenne was my fault, you know, because of the song. But after a while, with neither one of us talking, I kind of disappeared into the car radio. It was playing some New Wave crap—Culture Club, I think—I would never admit to liking in public, but in my head I was singing along.

"He asked me to leave." Chey's voice startled me. My nervous system was pulled right back to a state of high alert. Launch the bombers, flood the tubes, that sort of thing.

"Why?" It came out more as a croak than an actual word.

"He didn't say. But I think it was his leg?"

"His leg?"

"Yeah, when he got up to hug me, he lost his balance and pulled us both down onto the bed."

"Smooth move."

"It wasn't like that!" Chey snapped.

"Sorry," I muttered, and kept my eyes on the road.

"That's what he was afraid of, that I was thinking he was trying to get us to, you know. It never even crossed my mind. I could tell that he'd lost his balance and had just fallen."

"And he asked you to leave over that?"

"I think he was embarrassed. Embarrassed that he couldn't be there for me. He started crying, Harry. I've never seen Johnny cry. It was so awful."

I'd never seen Johnny cry, either. His default reaction to adversity was anger, not despair.

We were quiet for another minute; then I decided to go out on a ledge.

"Chey, why were you crying to begin with?"

CHEYENNE BELLE

When Harry asked me why I was crying, while we were tooling all over Westchester County in his car, I thought for a minute about telling him the truth. I felt like I needed to tell someone, but that seemed wrong to me. Johnny was the father, and he needed to know first. I would just have to figure it out, so I dodged the question.

"You know what we need?" I said instead. "We need to jam."

There is nothing in the world, not even kissing, that brings a smile to the face of Harbinger Jones like the phrase *We need to jam*. Of all of us, that boy's soul is most connected with the sacrament of music. Plus, playing a bunch of older Scar Boys tunes would wash away "Pleasant Sounds." As much as I loved that song, I needed to get it out of my brain.

Anyway, at the mention of jamming, Harry seemed to forget his question about why I'd been crying.

HARBINGER JONES

I didn't forget about the question. Chey made such a show of changing the topic so suddenly that I just let it drop.

CHEYENNE BELLE

It was too early for Richie to be home from school, so Harry and I went to the diner for lunch. I wasn't feeling so hot, so I didn't eat much, but we sat there for a long time. We didn't say a whole lot, but that was okay. One of things I love about Harry is that the silences between us are almost never awkward.

HARBINGER JONES

The silences between us are almost *always* awkward.

CHEYENNE BELLE

When we finally got to Richie's house he wasn't there. Mr. Mac, his dad, told us that he'd come home after school, grabbed his skateboard, and left. We thanked him and went to Richie's usual skating spot, the playground at PS 28, where Johnny and Richie went to grade school. (Even though they all lived close together, Harry was districted for a different school, PS some number I can't remember.)

Sure enough, Richie was there, just kind of skating in circles by himself. He had a Walkman on his hip and headphones on his ears.

We sat and watched for a minute from the car.

"I envy that," Harry said, as much to himself as to me.

"What do you mean?"

"Look at him. He's completely lost in the moment. It's like the world outside doesn't exist."

"And?"

"Don't you wish you could feel like that sometimes?"

"Who, me?"

"No. I mean, maybe. I guess I mean me."

I stared at him, thinking he must be kidding. When he looked over at me, I could see he was surprised.

"What?"

"Harry, have you ever seen yourself play the guitar?"

A flash of understanding made its way across his face, and he smiled. It's a weird and unusual smile, but I still think it's beautiful. He stepped out of the car to go get Richie.

I watched as Harry trudged to the playground. It's amazing how he looks completely normal from the back. I mean, that's got to be hard. Someone is behind you in line at the store, then you turn around, and wham!

Harry startled Richie, who fell off his board but laughed anyway. Harry helped him up, said something to him, and then they both looked at the car. Richie nodded and followed Harry back.

"What up, short stuff?" It was Richie's standard greeting for me. "Are we picking up Johnny, too?"

I didn't know what to say. Luckily, Harry did.

"John's not feeling so hot today, so we thought we would jam with just the three of us. You know, like in Athens."

Richie, being Richie, sat back and said, "Okay." And that was that.

When we got to Harry's house, Richie and I went to the basement while Harry went upstairs to talk to his mom about something. Richie took his seat behind the drums, and I sat down on my amp. I looked him in the eye.

Like I said earlier, Richie and I didn't talk much, so he wasn't really expecting anything from me. He was kind of in his own world when he noticed me staring him down.

"Yo," he said.

"Yo," I answered. "So what did Harry tell you about why we're jamming on our day off?"

He raised one eyebrow and said, "He just told me that you were in a place that you needed to jam. As you know, I can respect that."

"You didn't ask why?"

"Didn't need to. A dude—or dudette—needs to jam, you jam. Why, you pregnant or something?"

Holy crap, I was not expecting that, and it must've showed all over my face. I was too stunned to answer.

Richie was quiet for a moment while he looked at me like a puppy, with his head cocked to one side. Then he saw something—maybe it was my eyes, maybe it was my boobs, and, yeah, he looked there, too—that gave me away.

"Holy fuck," he said. "I was just kidding. For real, you're pregnant?" I nodded, and he paused a beat before asking, "Does Johnny know?"

"No! And neither does Harry, and you can't tell them, all right?"

He nodded. "Damn, you feeling okay?"

And you know what? Of the few people I'd told—Theresa, the priest—the only one who bothered to ask how I was feeling was Richie. Everyone else got lost in their own hang-ups. Theresa was still lost in the tragedy of her own experience, and the priest was lost in the rules of Mother Church. They both saw my pregnancy as their problem or their opportunity. Only Richie saw it as mine.

He isn't always the sharpest tool in the shed—I don't know, maybe that's not a fair thing to say; more like he's not always the most interested tool in the shed—but he's probably the most decent. It also felt really good and really scary that someone in the band knew.

RICHIE MCGILL

When Chey told me she was pregnant, I was completely freaking out on the inside. I mean, she was pregnant! I wanted to ask her all sorts of questions—Was she gonna keep it? How could she play bass when, you know, she got big and stuff? Could she feel it squirming around inside her?—but I didn't. I could tell she wanted her space, so I kept my trap shut. I'm pretty good at that. I guess that's why the other guys in the band tell me stuff. I'm good with secrets. I hate them, but I'm good with them.

CHEYENNE BELLE

When Harry came back into the room, you could feel the tension. It was like waves pounding a beach. He looked at me and Richie, waiting for us to say something.

Richie, true to his word, kept my secret. "C'mon," he said. "Let's make some noise." And we played.

For a little while, everything was great. It's always great when we play music. It's like it connects me to the rest of the world.

Have you ever held a bass guitar? If you have, then you know it's big. And it's heavy. Much bigger and heavier than regular guitars. And in case you haven't noticed, I'm small. Just holding the bass makes me feel gravity more than someone else does. The whole thing pulls me down to the earth. It's an incredible feeling. I'm rooted, stable.

But that's only the beginning. The real magic is when you plug it in.

Bass notes are low, rumbling, like the language mountains must use to talk to each other. It's like the instrument plants me on the ground, and then my fingers draw music up from the center of the earth.

It's hard to explain.

Anyway, we played for about forty-five minutes, and it felt good. But then the elephants in the room—my pregnancy, the fact that Richie knew about it, Harry's song, worry about Johnny—started to gather together and dance around me.

Plus, something wasn't feeling right. My back hurt and my stomach was starting to cramp. Time to go.

I told the guys I was tired and asked Harry to drive me home.

HARBINGER JONES

We dropped Richie at his house and then headed for Chey's.

"Cheyenne," I said when we were alone in the car, using her full name so she'd know I was serious. She didn't answer, and she didn't look good. She just waited for me to continue. "That song I wrote—"

"Harry," she cut me off, "don't. I can't—"

She looked like she was going to cry, and I wasn't sure

what to do, so I pulled over. We were on Central Avenue, near the racetrack.

Turns out I was reading her expression all wrong. Crying wasn't what she had in mind. For the second time in my life, Cheyenne Belle threw up all over me and my stuff.

If you've never been puked on, it's pretty disgusting. But for me, it wasn't about the vomit. The other time Chey threw up on me was also at the exact moment I tried to talk about my feelings for her. I know I'm repulsive, but this was the girl who'd kissed me. I can't be that repulsive, can I? The answer to that question, in case you're wondering, is a resounding yes.

Chey helped me clean up the mess, apologizing the whole time. We rolled down the windows and, even though it was cold out, blasted the AC to get the smell out as I drove the last couple of blocks to her house. She didn't say anything on the ride over or when she got out of the car. She just gave me a sad, backward glance. Like the Lorax.

CHEYENNE BELLE

I was pretty sure it wasn't morning sickness. That had more or less ended a couple of weeks before, and, besides, this felt different. It was more like puking from a fever, you know? I figured maybe I was getting the flu.

I felt really bad about the mess in Harry's car and did

my best to help him clean it up. Then he dropped me off at home.

My mother was bitching at me about something or other the second I walked through the door, but I just ignored her and went straight to my room and fell asleep.

I had this really vivid dream that I was being chased by a pair of sneakers. There wasn't anyone in them, just a pair of sneakers. I don't know why I was so terrified of them, but I was. That had to be the most restless sleep I've ever had.

HARBINGER JONES

I watched Chey get safely inside, and then I just started driving. I wasn't at all conscious of my surroundings.

It was a lot like this one night in Athens when everything felt like it was spinning out of control and I just walked aimlessly. I wound up at a phone booth downtown and called Dr. Kenny. That night, everything in the world was hyperreal. On this day, it all sort of disappeared.

By the time I'd zoned back in, I'd made it all the way to the Kensico Dam, like fifteen miles away. It was kind of scary that I'd driven that far without any real understanding of how I'd gone from point A to point B. I parked the car, got out, wandered into the dam's main plaza, and sat down on a low stone wall.

It was early November, it was gray, and it was getting cold. I wasn't dressed for the weather, but I was feeling numb and didn't really notice. I started listing all the things I couldn't control:

Thing I Couldn't Control #1:

I was never going to stop wanting Chey,

needing Chey, and loving Chey.

(Three out of three ain't bad,

either, Meat Loaf.)

Thing I Couldn't Control #2:

Cheyenne was never

going to love me back.

Thing I Couldn't Control #3:

Chey and Johnny were going

to be together forever.

I could feel the world disappearing even more, so I started on one of my lists to help me calm down. It was the periodic table, rearranged to put the elements in alphabetical order.

Actinium

Aluminum

Americium

It was starting to work; my heart was retreating from the redline. But something inside me made me stop. That kind of freaked me out, because once I got going on a list, I never stopped. Ever. But this time I just couldn't go any further.

Strike that. Not that I couldn't go any further; I didn't want to.

I was tired of the lists. Tired of preventing myself from feeling whatever it was the world wanted me to feel. Tired of walking through life anesthetized.

It's not an exaggeration to say that those lists saved my life. Without them, I would've spun out of control and broken down more than once. But now, sitting there on that wall, the massive stone dam looming over me like the personification of my fate, enough was enough.

No more lists. Something in my life needed to change.

PART FOUR.
NOVEMBER TO DECEMBER 1986

*Being in Fleetwood Mac is more like
being in group therapy.*

—Mick Fleetwood

Who do you really admire and/or want to emulate?

HARBINGER JONES

The answer for me has always been Lucky Strike the Lightning Man. He's this guy who was struck by lightning—unlike me, he was actually struck by lightning instead of almost struck by lightning—but rather than letting it ruin his life, he turned it into something positive. He became an expert in meteorology, and he helped other lightning-strike victims. He really helped me when I was a little kid, and I'm forever in his debt.

CHEYENNE BELLE

Johnny McKenna.

RICHIE MCGILL

The Bay City Rollers.
    Just kidding.
    My dad.

CHEYENNE BELLE

I woke up the next morning with a sharp pain in my gut and I was clammy and sweating. Throwing the covers off my body made the pain even more intense, and I moaned.

It was Saturday morning, and Theresa and Agnes were both still in bed.

Right away, Theresa could see something was wrong.

"Chey?" she asked, propping herself up.

"I don't feel good." I clutched my stomach and moaned again. I stayed on my bed, curled up on my side like a fetus. And, yeah, I get the irony. I guess it's what all people do when the world—because of pain or sadness or something else—becomes too much to bear; we try our hardest to find a way to crawl back into the womb.

"Cheyenne, I think you need a tampon." Agnes was very matter-of-fact.

"Huh?"

"You're bleeding."

"Shit," Theresa said, rushing over to me.

I think I yelped or cried out, I'm not sure.

"What's going on?" Agnes had only just turned sixteen, but somehow she seemed older than Theresa and me. She was a straight-A student, treasurer of the sophomore class at Our Lady of the Perpetual Adoration Academy—the same high school I'd barely graduated from a few months before—and she played, well, I don't know how many sports. I lost count. Agnes even had a job as a cashier at Wanamaker's.

She was confident, tender, and funny, and she was my favorite Belle girl. I was the bigger sister, but, really, I looked up to Agnes.

Theresa tensed up and looked at me. Agnes must've sensed it, because she looked at both of us and said, "Seriously, what's going on?"

"Nothing," I answered. "It's just my period. Can we let it go?" But I was feeling too crappy and was too freaked out for Agnes to buy my excuse. In that moment I don't think I could've convinced a three-year-old that Santa Claus was real.

Agnes waited a beat, looking from me to Theresa and back again. Theresa was staring at the floor, which was a pretty obvious sign that something was wrong.

"Wait, are you pregnant?" Agnes didn't know how loud her voice was.

Theresa and I both shushed her.

"If Mom and Dad find out, they're going to kill you!"

"I know," Theresa said, shushing her again, "which is why we need you to keep it down."

Agnes nodded and then looked at me. "But why are you bleeding if you're pregnant?"

I started crying.

"C'mon," Theresa said, taking charge. "We're getting you to an emergency room. Now."

"But Mom and Dad can't find out," I blubbered.

"Fine. We can go to Planned Parenthood. It's cheaper, and they won't call home."

They helped me up and got my clothes off. There was a lot of blood. Well, not all blood. I don't really know what you'd call it. It was a brownish, reddish, stickyish fluid, and it smelled awful. It smelled like death. I thought I was going to throw up again.

My two sisters—my two younger sisters, both still teenagers and both still in high school—helped clean me up. They loaded a fresh pair of panties with so many pads that I could barely walk. Agnes gave me a pair of her sweatpants and a loose-fitting shirt, and we left.

HARBINGER JONES

When I finally got up the next day, it was almost 11:00 a.m. I'd stayed up late the night before, leafing through this thick paperback guide to colleges that had been lying around my house since I'd been a sophomore in high school. My dad had given it to me in this big show of what he thought was moral support. Where my mom always surprised me with fun presents, like a new comic book or a package of blank cassette tapes, my dad would lie in wait with college guides and articles from the *New England Journal of Medicine* on the latest advances in plastic surgery, like that was supposed to make me feel better.

But the more I looked at that guide, the more I liked the idea of college. I don't know if college was exactly what I had in mind when I started thinking about a life change, but it made sense. Applying would make my parents happy, and like it was for so many other people, attending would be the path of least resistance.

It was fun to read about all the different programs of study offered; fun to read the sections called "campus life" and imagine myself fitting in somehow, and fun to lose myself in the student population totals, the number of applicants versus the number accepted, and the outrageous tuition costs.

I had made notes in the margins back when I was thinking of applying the first time. Leafing through the second time, after I'd been out of high school for six months, I saw what an amazing exercise in self-delusion a book like that can be. I had notes next to Yale, Brown, and Cornell. Until you start sending out applications, the possibilities are limitless and they are real. It's kind of like Schrödinger's cat. The college has neither accepted nor rejected you until you apply.

Of course, the listings also showed what grades and SAT scores you needed to get in, so maybe the cat was more dead than alive. For the record, my grades sucked. Like, Hoover-vacuum-cleaner sucked. As for my SATs, well, let's just say that both the reading and math scores started with a four. I couldn't have even gotten into Transylvania University if I tried. And, yes, there really is a school called Transylvania University. It's in Kentucky. You can look it up.

CHEYENNE BELLE

I was feeling so bad and so scared that I don't really even remember how we got to the clinic. I know we took a cab, but I don't remember the drive there at all.

When I stepped onto the curb I was pulled back to reality because, of course, there were protesters. Just a handful, which I suppose isn't bad for a Saturday morning, but it was enough. They were in our faces the second the cab pulled away.

Some were women, some men, all of them yelling at us. They were like a disorganized pack of wild dogs.

"You fucking whore," one old bat screamed.

"Don't listen to her, child," a middle-aged man said. "But don't confound the sin of fornication with the sin of murder."

"Just ignore them," Agnes whispered in my ear. She locked arms with me on one side, Theresa on the other.

Just before we got to the last part of the walkway— I don't think the protesters were legally allowed to go right up to the door—this Stepford wife jumped in front of me, holding what was supposed to be a fetus in a jar of red liquid.

"Please," she begged us. "Please don't do this. Don't do what I did."

I think she wanted us to believe she was holding her own aborted fetus. My adrenaline kicked in, because for a minute I forgot about the pain and forgot to be scared. I defaulted to my usual emotion when things weren't going right: anger. Without really thinking, I wrestled my arm free from Agnes and I shoved the woman.

I didn't mean for her to fall, but she did. Everyone gasped, even me. Theresa tried to catch the jar as it floated up in the air, but she couldn't. It landed hard on the walkway and shattered.

The woman yelped like a coyote and, with lightning speed, gathered up her fetus. But not before I could see that it was a plastic fake. We just stepped around her and went inside.

"You fucking bitches!" she screamed after us. My sisters had to stop me from turning around and kicking her.

The waiting room was small. There were half a dozen chairs, a small pile of magazines on a coffee table, and pamphlets and posters everywhere about reproductive systems and reproductive rights. There were two other people there: a girl about my age reading a book called

Crossing to Safety, and a guy in his thirties holding a clipboard. I figured he worked there.

"Hi," he said, coming up to us before we were all the way in the room.

I was too out of it to answer, so Agnes took charge.

"Hello," she answered. "My sister needs to see a doctor right away."

"Oh," he said as his face went flush. "I'm sorry, I don't work for Planned Parenthood. You need to check in at the desk." He nodded to the registration area, which was basically a wall of what I guessed was bulletproof glass with a small sliding window. An older and tired-looking woman sat behind it, watching the four of us.

"So what," Theresa snapped at the man, "are the fucking protestors coming inside now?"

"What? No, no. I'm not a protestor." The guy, who had jet-black hair and the bushiest eyebrows I've ever seen, was knocked way off his game. "I'm here working for Planned Parenthood, registering gir—women, I mean registering women, to vote."

Agnes, Theresa, and I looked at each other. My sisters burst out laughing. If I hadn't felt like I was going to die, I might've laughed, too.

"Yeah, Mister," Theresa said. "I'm sure all the girls coming in here"—and she underlined *girls*—"are in the right frame of mind to perform their civic duty or whatever."

I was feeling worse by the second, so I touched Theresa's arm. She looked at me and understood right away.

She brushed past the guy, maybe a little rougher than she needed to, and escorted me to the desk.

The room was too small for the guy to get far enough away from us, so he called out to the woman behind the glass that he was taking a break and left through the front door.

"Don't be too hard on him, girls," the woman said, and she underlined the word, too. "He's actually donating his time to help raise awareness about what we do here. As long as we have those lunatics out front, we need people like him in here. Now, does one of you have an appointment?"

"No," Agnes said. "My sister is—how pregnant are you?" she asked me.

"I don't know. I think about four months."

"My sister is four months pregnant, and she's bleeding a lot. And her stomach hurts a lot."

The woman, who had been calm, almost sleepy, sat up straight. She pushed a clipboard at Agnes through the glass window. "Fill this out for your sister. And you," she said to me, "come with me."

"Can one of my sisters come, too?" I asked, my voice a squeak as another wave of pain hit me. Theresa, who still had her arm locked through mine, gripped tighter.

HARBINGER JONES

An eighteen-year-old kid applying to college shouldn't be a big deal, but for me, it was.

When the band was gearing up for our first tour, during my senior year of high school, I lied to my parents and told them I'd been accepted at the University of Scranton, that I would be attending in the fall. I hadn't even applied. It was a pretty elaborate lie—I forged all the admission documents and pretended to mail my dad's check to the school—and I rode it all the way to the end, until I got caught. My parents did not take it well. The idea of college now was, for me, like a career criminal deciding to go straight.

When I was leafing through the guide, I thought for a little while about applying to music colleges, like Berklee in Boston or Julliard in New York. But I wasn't that kind of musician. I didn't read music, didn't really want to read music, and didn't have any interest in a career playing wicked guitar solos on television commercials for deodorants and cat litter.

And because I didn't have a backup plan, I didn't have a clue as to what colleges to target. So I applied to the only school that made sense: the University of Scranton, my fake alma mater. Maybe this time I could get in for real. I still had a clean copy of their admissions package—once you're on a school's mailing list, they send you lots of the same stuff over and over again—so I took it out and went to work.

The application was pretty straightforward, and it only took an hour to complete, except for the essay. I can't tell you how many times I started and stopped writing that stupid thing.

Each time my pencil hit the paper, the essay came out as really dry, boring crap about what a great student I'd be. I read and reread the instructions and kept getting hung up on the word count. I was supposed to tell them something interesting about me in two hundred and fifty words or less. Two hundred and fifty words!

I tried to take a fresh eye to the instructions and shifted my focus. This was what I landed on:

YOUR PERSONAL ESSAY WILL

HELP US BECOME

ACQUAINTED WITH YOU BEYOND YOUR COURSES,

GRADES, AND TEST SCORES.

They wanted to know who I really was.

So who am I? I thought. *I'm the guitar player in a thrashing, smashing, ass-kicking punk rock band, but I'm also a disfigured monster with all kinds of crazy social anxiety, and I'm an almost-twenty-year-old virgin who has kissed exactly one girl, and that kiss lasted for all of five seconds.* But when I really thought about who I was, about what I could tell them to help them know me beyond my dismal grades and test scores, I kept coming back to the same thing.

I, Harbinger Robert Francis Jones, am a coward.

CHEYENNE BELLE

The doctor's room was cold, not just the temperature, but the aura, too. Sometimes, a place can just give off waves of coldness, you know? I was told to take off my clothes, put on a paper-thin gown, and lie down on the examination table. I noticed that the cushion on the table was graying with age and cracking at the seams.

"I'm still bleeding," I said, embarrassed that I was going to make a mess. The woman went into a closet and pulled out what looked like a giant maxipad, or maybe a maxipad for a giant. Almost like what you would use to house-train a puppy.

"It's okay," she said. "We're a gynecological office. Lots of our patients bleed."

I nodded and did what I was told.

The woman waited for Agnes to finish filling out the forms and took the clipboard back. "The doctor will be right in." And she left.

"Are you doing okay?" Agnes asked while we waited for the doctor.

I wasn't doing okay. I was still bleeding; my gut felt like someone was trying to wring it dry, like a washcloth after a shower; and I was suddenly hit with the thought that I had no idea how we were going to pay for any of this.

Agnes, who, like I said, is the most mature one of us, must've read my mind.

"Don't worry about the money," she said. "I have a lot saved. You can pay me back."

"I can give you some, too," Theresa said. I didn't think Theresa had any money, and I didn't think she really wanted to give it to me, but Agnes's generosity had shamed her into making the offer.

It's not that Agnes shamed her on purpose. It's that girls like Theresa and me just sort of start out from a place of feeling shame. I don't know if that makes sense, but it's the truth.

Anyway, it didn't matter. They had both offered, and it calmed me down, at least a little bit, and it made me love my sisters more than I ever had before.

Then a new woman came in, this one wearing a white lab coat.

"I'm Dr. McCartney," she said. "You must be"—and she looked down at the clipboard—"Cheyenne."

I was surprised that the doctor was a woman. I've been so trained to think of doctors as men that it never occurred to me that this doctor would be anything else. It made me happy.

"Yes."

"It's a nice name. So tell me what's going on." She was young, and she had dark brown hair that was pulled back in a ponytail and charcoal-colored bags under her eyes, almost like she'd got beaten up.

"I'm pregnant, and I think something's going wrong." I told her as much detail as I could about the bleeding and the cramps.

"Okay. Are you a patient of the clinic or do you have another OB/GYN?"

"This is my first trip to a doctor."

"How long ago was your last period?" Concern etched itself into the corner of her mouth.

"I don't know, like three or four months ago."

Dr. McCartney froze and looked from me to Theresa.

"Are you sure?"

I knew enough to be embarrassed about not having come to the doctor sooner, so I just hung my head and nodded.

The doctor, who was probably used to seeing dumb little girls like me, forced a smile.

"Okay, then, let's see what we're dealing with." She pulled a rolling stool up next to the examination table and grabbed a plastic tube of Vaseline. "This is going to be a bit cold." She squirted a bunch on my stomach, and it was cold. It made me flinch, which made me hurt.

With my shirt off, you could see the barest hint of the bump that was my baby trying to push its way out of my belly. The doctor took out this flat black paddle thing, which was hooked up to a machine with what looked like a telephone cord. Like one of those things they use to start your heart when it stops.

Seeing that freaked me out. But the paddle wasn't for hearts. It was for sonograms. Agnes, Theresa, and I watched the grainy black-and-white TV monitor as the doctor moved the paddle all around my stomach. The room was quiet, and my attention wandered from the monitor to the doctor's face.

Every muscle in her jaw and neck had pulled itself tight, and her forehead was scrunched. After one last go-round with the paddle, she bit her lower lip, pushed her stool back, and looked at me.

"What?" I asked.

The doctor put the paddle back in its holder and took my hands. She looked me straight in the eye.

"I'm sorry, Cheyenne," she said, choosing her words carefully. "There's no heartbeat. You're having a miscarriage."

One of my sisters gasped—I'm not sure which one—and at first, I didn't know why. Dr. McCartney kept holding my hands and watching, waiting for me to catch up.

I did.

No heartbeat.

My baby was dead.

HARBINGER JONES

I'm a socially awkward, disfigured, guitar-playing coward. Try to tell *that* story in two hundred and fifty words or less. It can't be done. I mean, it literally can't be done. I know. I tried. At least twenty times I tried.

I finally decided that I should just ignore the word count in the Scranton essay instructions and get everything I could think of down on paper. Then I could go back and edit later.

I had this English teacher in high school who liked to say that "all good writing is rewriting." I didn't know what that meant at the time—if she hadn't taken pity on me, I think I would have failed her class—but now I understood. The musical equivalent is "We'll fix it in the mix." When you record music, you try not to worry too much about equalization or effects when you're laying down basic tracks. You just need to make sure the performances are good. Anything else can be corrected when you mix all the tracks down to the master. Fix it in the mix.

I didn't know where to start my story, so I started with the obvious: the day I got these scars, the day I was tied to a tree during the thunderstorm. At first it was hard to drag those memories back to the surface. I'd spent a lifetime trying to bury and forget them, like they were the bones of someone I'd murdered. But the more I wrote, the more I needed to write.

I filled pages with details of the storm and the aftermath of being severely burned: the endless medical tests and procedures, how other kids treated me, all that time I spent with Dr. Kenny.

By the time I got to the part of my narrative where I met Johnny, in middle school, the pencil was flying across the page. I remembered every detail like it was yesterday. I could still see the bully—Billy the Behemoth—who Johnny stood up to on my behalf. I could still see Johnny's eyes staring Billy down.

I finished writing that scene and put the pencil on my desk. *Maybe,* I thought, *the story of my life is really the story of my friendship with Johnny.* I never had any siblings, and Johnny was like an unofficial brother. And like all brothers, we loved each other as much as we resented each other.

But did our relationship really define me? Was I so dependent on Johnny that my life didn't have meaning without him?

No. There was something else besides Johnny. Something bigger. Much bigger.

I smiled as I picked up the pencil again. It felt good to write. Felt good to get so much of it out of me. After a while, the writing wasn't even about Scranton. The exercise became its own reward.

CHEYENNE BELLE

A late-term miscarriage was what the doctor called it. Anything before twenty weeks—and we figured out that I was sixteen weeks—is a miscarriage. Anything after is a stillbirth. That's what they told us.

I just lay there and cried. The doctor left the room so my sisters and I could have a few minutes. I don't know how long I cried, but it was a long time.

I had only just decided to keep the baby, but maybe I'd been leaning that way all along. I mean, I'm definitely pro-choice and all—who am I or anyone else to tell girls what to think or what to do with their bodies—but given who I am and how I was raised, I don't know if I could've made any other decision. It was my *choice* to keep the baby. I mean, think about the words to "Lullaby." Of course I was going to keep the baby.

By that point, though, none of that stuff mattered.

The doctor's words—*There's no heartbeat*—were stuck in my brain like a skipping record. What the hell was I supposed to do with that?

Once I calmed myself down enough, I had only one thought. I squeezed Theresa's hand and said, "Get it out of me." She nodded and went to get the doctor.

An hour later, after more paperwork, after Agnes went home to get her money and had come back, the doctor was administering a local anesthetic.

The procedure for getting a dead baby out of you is pretty much the same as for an abortion. Either way, it's fucking awful. It's called a D & C. I didn't want to know anything about it, but Agnes kept asking questions.

"What does that stand for?"

"Dilation and curettage."

"What do you actually do?"

"We'll dilate Cheyenne's cervix and then remove the entire contents of her uterus."

"How?"

The doctor was explaining all this while she was doing other things to prep for the procedure. She reminded me of Richie's dad, Mr. Mac, who never seemed to have a moment when he wasn't doing something.

"We use something called a cannula tube. It creates a gentle suction that allows us to draw out any tissue."

I couldn't help but notice that she never referred to what was inside me as a baby.

"Wait," Theresa said. "You mean you, like, use a vacuum cleaner to suck the baby out of her? Gross!" Agnes looked at Theresa like she was going to kill her.

"Okay, girls, time for you to go to the waiting room," the doctor said abruptly. "This will take about thirty minutes, and the anesthesia is going to make Cheyenne feel a bit woozy. She'll need your help getting home."

"Of course, Doctor," Agnes said. Theresa rolled her

eyes at Agnes's perfect way of speaking, and then the doctor and I were alone.

"Does the father know?" she asked me as she started the process of dilation.

"What? Oh, no. I can't tell him."

Dr. McCartney looked at me. "Did he hurt you?"

The sedative was starting to kick in, and it took me a minute to understand what she was getting at.

"Hurt me?"

"Is that why you can't tell him?"

"No, no, it's not like that at all. He was in an accident a couple of months ago and lost his leg. He's dealing with his own shit. Sorry." I corrected myself, "Stuff."

The doctor smiled at me and went back to her work.

"Can I ask you something?" I asked.

"Shoot," she said.

"Johnny, the dad, stood up without his prosthetic leg, lost his balance, and fell on top of me yesterday. We landed on a bed. It wasn't too hard or anything, but could that have made this happen?" I couldn't keep the fear out of my voice.

"No, Cheyenne," she answered. "I don't think so. It would have to have been a pretty big trauma to your body, and what you're describing doesn't really fit the bill."

"Then why did this happen?" I started crying again.

"Look." She held my hand. "There could be lots of

medical reasons, some of them hereditary—"

I chuckled under my breath, but loud enough to cut the doctor off. "My mom has seven children, all girls," I explained, and then remembered that wasn't the whole story. "But my sister Theresa lost a baby last year. It was a stillbirth, at home, in bed."

"That could be an indicator of the hereditary nature of what's happening here. Is your sister okay?"

"Actually, she's usually a pretty big bitch." Dr. McCartney smiled but didn't play along with the lame joke I was trying to make. Given how nice Theresa was being, I knew it was a pretty crappy thing to say. "Maybe that's harsh," I added, trying to redeem myself. "I mean, she's here now. That's more than I've ever done for her." I paused before adding, "Maybe I'm the bitch." Dr. McCartney chuckled with me at first, but noticed almost right away that my laughter was morphing into sobs. I was totally losing it.

Squeezing my hand one more time and letting it go, the doctor went back to work while she talked to me. "There are genetic markers that we're only just now beginning to understand. But like so much of what can go wrong with the human body, sometimes there is no rhyme or reason. It is what it is. That doesn't make it better or easier, but it also doesn't preclude you from having children someday in the future—far in the future. Speaking of which, you should probably make an appointment to come back and talk to me about birth control."

I nodded and was quiet.

Other than little words of explanation ("You might feel a little pinch") or encouragement ("You're doing great, Cheyenne"), Dr. McCartney didn't talk again until it was finished.

"Your body's been through a lot, and I want you to get rest. I'm going to give you a prescription for pain medicine and one for antibiotics. Take the pain meds as you need them, but be sure to finish the entire flight of antibiotics." She took my hand, squeezed it, and looked me square in the eye. "You're going to be fine, you understand? You have a good family. Let them take care of you.

"Stay here for a few minutes," she said as she stood up. "I'll send your sisters in."

She left the room. I muttered, "Thank you," to an afterimage of Dr. McCartney and started crying again.

HARBINGER JONES

I told my parents I wasn't feeling well and ate dinner in my room. I wanted to keep working on the essay, and I didn't want them to know what I was doing. I was pretty sure they would both completely freak out, especially my dad, and that wasn't what I needed just then. I wasn't even sure that I actually wanted to go to college. I mean, the idea was more and more appealing, but I wanted to keep my options open. For now this would stay my secret.

I wrote until my vision was blurred and my hand was so cramped I could barely hold the pencil. It was 3:00 a.m. when I stopped, and dozens of notebook pages were filled, front and back. I got all the way to the moment in the story of my life when Johnny suggested we start a band.

The more I thought about that moment, about me and him in his house, listening to records and talking about music, the more I realized that was the moment my life really began. So I used my cramped hand to scratch, *And that was how it all began,* onto the page before finally stopping for the night.

Take that, admissions professional, I thought. *I'm already so far over your word count as to be ridiculous, and now I'm telling you that I haven't even started yet.*

For some reason, I thought that was really funny, and for the very first time in my life that I could remember, I fell asleep giggling.

CHEYENNE BELLE

I took one of the pain meds, took my antibiotics, and slept that night at home like I'd never slept before. When I woke up the next day, a Sunday, my parents and most of my sisters had gone to church. Only Theresa and I were in the house.

She was in bed when I rolled over and opened my eyes. "Am I still cool with Mom and Dad?"

Theresa was lying there with her Walkman on, listening to God-knows-what-awful pop music—Debbie Gibson or Madonna or something. Her favorite song, which she played all the time, was "All You Zombies" by the Hooters. It has to be the dumbest song ever recorded. Did you know that that band put it out as a single not once, but twice, and that they included it on two different albums? Way to beat a dead horse, guys.

Anyway, Theresa didn't hear me, so I took off my sock to throw at her, you know, to get her attention. Only when I bent over, my midsection really hurt.

I knew I'd moaned, but I didn't realize how loud until Theresa sat up and dropped her headphones to her neck.

"Are you all right?"

"I think so," I said, out of breath. "Is it supposed to hurt this much?"

"Yes," she answered, slid the headphones up, and lay back down. I guess things were back to normal between us.

I still had a sock in my hand, so I threw it at her anyway.

"What the fuck, Cheyenne?" She was back up, and the headphones were back down.

"I don't know, maybe a little support?" It was the wrong thing to say.

"A little support? Are you kidding?"

"Look, I—"

"No, you look. Aggie and I talked last night after you passed out. This cost us a lot of money." I hated that people called my sister Aggie. I knew she didn't like it, because when people outside the family used that nickname, she always set them straight. But it was too late with Theresa; that ship sailed when Agnes—which is such a pretty name—was three.

"I'm gonna pay you back." I don't know what I'd expected when I woke up, but it wasn't getting yelled at.

"With what, the money for your little band of weirdos and cripples?" When she wanted to, Theresa could be the biggest bitch on the planet. I was too weak to fight back, so I laid my head down and closed my eyes. The connection I'd had with my sisters the day before felt so real and so nice, but it was like a temporary tattoo that had worn off overnight.

"I'll get a job," I said without any emotion. Theresa snorted.

I lay there for another minute before the sock I'd thrown at Theresa came back and hit me in the face. I sat up and looked at her. Something in her face had softened a little.

"Look, if there's anyone in the world who knows how you feel, it's me, and I'm sorry if I sound like a bitch." I didn't answer. I think maybe she was waiting for me to tell her that it was okay, that she wasn't a bitch, but that wasn't going to happen, so I just kept my mouth shut until she finished. "But you'll get over this. You're not the first girl to lose a baby, and you won't be the last."

I guess that was Theresa's way of telling me everything was going to be okay. Pretty lame, right? Anyway, I just nodded and put my head back down.

I don't know if my sister heard or saw me crying—I tried to be quiet, and I figured that she had put the headphones back on—but I refused to open my eyes to find out. I fell back asleep.

When I finally got up, after my family got back from church, my mother scolded me for sleeping so late. "When the Lord made Sunday a day of rest, he didn't make it for you." I was actually happy to hear it. It meant she didn't know anything about what had happened the day before.

I told her that I was sick and was going back to bed. She just snorted at me. I called Johnny and told him the same thing.

"I'm sorry about the other day," he said. His voice sounded far away and sad, like that donkey from *Winnie-the-Pooh*.

I was confused and paranoid for a minute, and thought maybe he'd found out about Planned Parenthood and was apologizing for not being there.

"Yeah, you know, in my bedroom."

Then it hit me. He was talking about falling on top of me on his bed. Did that happen only Friday? I was disoriented and freaked out. I told him not to worry about it, but that I really wasn't feeling well and that I needed to sleep.

"Okay, Pick," he said. "Let me know if I can bring you anything."

"Thanks," I answered.

"I love you." We'd been saying that to each other since the summer, and it had become our standard way of saying good-bye. When you say something over and over, it starts to lose its meaning. It doesn't carry any more weight than *adios, ciao,* or *see you later.* It becomes a noise, a kind of emotional grunt, you know?

But this time it had all the meaning in the world, and I choked up. I pretended to cough, said, "I love you," back, and hung up the phone, burying my face in my pillow when I did.

I knew then that I could never tell Johnny that I'd carried and lost his baby, our baby. He just wouldn't understand why I'd kept it from him in the first place. If I could go back in time and do one thing over, it would be that phone call. I would just tell Johnny everything.

"Smooth," Theresa said from the doorway. That was the thing about my house. You never could get any privacy.

I gave her the finger and laid my head gently down on the pillow.

RICHIE MCGILL

Yeah, the band went on a minibreak when Chey "got the flu." I knew she was pregnant, and I was worried something was going on. I kind of wanted to call and ask how she was doing, but that's not how we rolled.

I wound up spending a lot of that week just hanging around at home after school. The weather got way colder, and I wasn't really in the mood to take my board out, so I watched TV, drank iced tea and ate party pretzels, and practiced drumming on my pads.

And then Johnny called.

Johnny never called me. None of the guys in the band ever really called me. It's something about being a drummer. Guitar players and singers and bass players all think we're some sort of spare part: like we're spark plugs, easy to replace. That's why there are so many drummer jokes.

What happened when the bass player locked his keys in the car? It took him half an hour to get the drummer out. There's, like, a million of them, and they all pretty much make drummers out to be idiots. It doesn't really bug me, though. I mean, I notice, but I figure it's someone else's hang-up, not mine.

So anyways, Johnny calls and says that since the band isn't jamming, he wants to hang out, and can I come pick him up?

"Sure," I say.

"Great," he says, sounding really relieved or something. "Bring your skateboard."

My board? I think to myself, but I don't question it. Johnny'd seemed a bit, I don't know, out of tune, and I figured I should try to help him.

So fifteen minutes later I'm at his house, his mother showing me to his bedroom. I'd been before, but not that often, so I could feel his mom kind of checking me out. I don't mean checking me out 'cause she wanted to see my hot ass, I mean sizing me up. We all knew she hated Harry and Cheyenne—even Johnny said that was true—but she didn't really know me. I was pretty sure she didn't like me any better, because, you know, I was in the band.

When I walked into Johnny's room, he was downing a pill of some sort with a glass of water.

"What's that, for your leg?"

He looked at me for a long moment, embarrassed, I think, that I'd caught him taking meds.

"Antidepressant," he said, and then added, "Don't tell Chey or Harry, okay? It's not a big deal, and I know both of them would make it a big deal."

He was right about that; they would. So I agreed.

"How long you supposed to take them for?"

"I don't know. Until I'm not depressed, I guess."

"Why are you depressed?" He looked at me, looked at

his leg, and held out his arms as if to say, "Why the fuck do you think I'm depressed, numb nuts?"

"Yeah, okay," I said. "I get it. But, John, when you think about it, things could be a lot worse."

He just rolled his eyes and asked, "Did you bring your board?"

"Yeah, it's in the car."

"Good."

"Why?"

"I want you to teach me to ride."

"Say what?"

"Look, I need to do something to push myself harder. I see how much you love it, and figure it's a good way to test the boundaries of my leg."

"I don't know, John. . . ."

"C'mon, I'll be fine. It'll be fun."

"It's a little cold for skateboarding." I thought this was a bad idea, and I was trying to make any excuse to get out of it.

"We have coats. Let's go."

That was Johnny at his best. The case was closed, and we were going. He had this weird voodoo shit that made you go along. It's how I joined the band in the first place.

I was in the seventh grade and had just gotten this used, piece-of-crap, three-piece drum set for my birthday. I couldn't play for shit. Anyway, Johnny, who was a year older than me, had somehow heard about it. He found me at my locker.

I knew who Johnny was. Everyone in our school did. He was one of those dudes who seemed to be at the center of things.

"You're Richie," he said to me. "You play drums."

"Yeah," I answered, not sure what to make of the fact that Johnny McKenna had singled me out.

"I'm starting a band, and we need a drummer. You're it. I'll let you know when and where our first practice is."

That was it. No invitation to join, just an order to follow. And like everyone else who dealt with Johnny, I just went along. Best thing that ever happened to me.

Anyways, back to the day he called me. A few minutes later, we were on the playground at our old elementary school and Johnny was using his good leg to push my skateboard while he stood on it with his fake leg. But here's the thing about skateboarding that most people don't realize: it's as much about your feet and ankles as it is about your legs. You make a million little adjustments every second just to stay on the board. I'm not saying someone with a fake leg can't learn to skateboard, but it would take time and maybe something better than the uneven elementary school blacktop on a cold November day.

Johnny kept falling off. Or the board would slide out from under his feet. Or it would flip up in the air and nail him in the crotch. (I laughed pretty hard when that happened.) But he kept at it. I tried to give him pointers, and at first he listened, but then he tuned me out. His face was getting redder and redder, and his muscles were getting all stiff, which is the worst thing for skateboarding.

Finally, after he'd fallen, like, twenty times, I knew I needed to pull the plug.

"John, I'm freezing my fucking ass off out here. Can we try this again in the spring?"

His face was a blank wall. He looked at me from the ground and just nodded. I went to help him up, but he batted my hand away.

I took him home, and that was that.

CHEYENNE BELLE

The experience of losing the baby—I can say those words now, but I couldn't back then—tore me up inside, both physically and mentally. I felt like someone had taken a razor blade and made tiny cuts all over my heart and all over my gut. I couldn't talk to anyone about it except for my sisters, and because of all the shit Theresa had said to me, I couldn't really even talk to them.

Every time I thought of the baby, of what he would have looked like (in my mind it was a boy), of how much I would've loved him, every time I wondered if the baby suffered when he died, I would start to unravel. I was like a cassette where the tape pulls loose, and the more you pull on it, the harder it gets to put back together.

Not sure of where else to turn, two days after the miscarriage and a week before we jammed again, I found myself back in the confessional.

"Bless me, Father, for I have sinned."

"Confess your sins to me, my child." I recognized the voice right away. This was the same priest I'd talked to last time.

"I gave confession a few weeks ago, Father, and told you about a friend of mine, who had gotten pregnant."

There was a long pause before he answered. "I remember, my child. What did your friend decide to do?"

"She decided to keep the baby, Father." It was somehow easier talking about this like it had happened to someone else. It put distance between me and the reality of what I was going through.

"That's good, that's good." I could hear the relief in his voice.

"And then she had a miscarriage. In her sixteenth week of pregnancy."

There was absolute silence on the other side of the little booth, not even breathing. That, more than anything, pissed me off.

"Really, Father? Nothing? No words of calming wisdom? No explanation for why, when this girl followed your advice, God swooped in and killed the baby in her uterus?" I used the word *uterus* on purpose, thinking it would make him uncomfortable.

"It is not for us to understand the ways of the Lor—"

I cut him off. "Is that really the best you've got? That 'whole-mystery-of-the-Lord' shit?" I don't think I'd ever cursed at, in front of, or even near a priest before, but I was too far gone to care. I think I might have been crying or screaming or both. "If this God of yours is so merciful and loving, why would he kill this girl's baby? Was it some kind of holy abortion? How do you explain this? Tell me!"

Again, he was quiet for a long moment before he whispered more than spoke, "I can't. It's a tragedy."

That jolted me back to the moment. I was bracing for more of the "God is mysterious" mumbo jumbo, and I hadn't expected him to say anything so honest. I lost it for real. I started crying and couldn't stop. Everything hurt so bad.

After a few minutes of me sitting there, blubbering, the door to the confessional opened, making me jump. And there he was, a short, fat priest with a ring of sandy-colored hair around his bald head. He was crying, too. He took my hand, led me out of the booth, and hugged me.

It was a long hug, and it was filled with sympathy and love. For a minute it even made me feel better. I think that priest violated every church rule to break down the wall of anonymity that was supposed to be between us, and I loved him for it.

I pulled myself together, backed away, and ran out of the church.

As surprising and tender as that moment was, and as good as crying and being hugged made me feel, it didn't fix me. And that's the problem with religion. A quick fix never works.

HARBINGER JONES

Chey's flu lasted a whole week. It was the longest we'd gone without rehearsing since we all reconnected after Georgia. It was also the longest we'd gone without seeing each other.

Something wasn't right about Cheyenne. She was, and I can't believe I'm going to use this word, boring. Cheyenne's always been an enthusiastic person—or wait, maybe that's not the right word, maybe *passionate* is better, passionate with an edge. When we got back to rehearsal, Cheyenne was morose. I chalked it up to a remnant of her being sick.

RICHIE MCGILL

Soon as I saw Chey at that rehearsal, I knew she wasn't pregnant anymore. I don't know how I knew, but I knew. She looked a little sad or something and like maybe she was a little stoned. I figured she'd had an abortion. That's what most girls our age would've done.

I caught her eye when she was walking in, and she gave me this little nod, like, "Yeah, it's done, and I'm all right." I let it go, but I kind of kept an eye on her during the rehearsal. She was quiet but okay, so I didn't push it.

HARBINGER JONES

"Feeling better?" I asked Chey as she plugged into her amp.

"Yeah, and sorry again about your car."

"What happened to your car?" Johnny looked at the two of us, confused. That took me by surprise. It was like Johnny and Cheyenne hadn't seen each other or even talked since the day I'd played "Pleasant Sounds" in Johnny's room, more than a week earlier. If that was true, it was unprecedented.

I was deep into writing my essay at that point and had detached myself from the rest of the world. I probably needed to be a better friend to Johnny, but I don't think I knew how. He hadn't been himself since the accident, but he'd settled into a predictable kind of pattern. He was quieter, maybe a bit depressed, but still even-keeled and in control. That first rehearsal back after Chey's flu bug, he looked like he was going to cry. It was noticeable enough that I asked him to come outside with me while I had a cigarette.

"You okay?"

"Me? Yeah, why?"

"I don't know. You just don't seem yourself."

"I think I'm just tired is all," he answered. I couldn't tell if he was hiding something or if he was really just tired. "Hey," he added, "did you talk to Chey during this past week?"

"No, why, didn't you?"

"She called to tell me she had the flu, but that was it." My suspicions were confirmed.

"I think she was pretty sick," I offered. "She puked all over my car."

"Yeah," he said. "I'm sure that's it. How about you?"

"Huh?"

"Everything okay with you?"

"I think so," I said. "Why?"

"I know you, Harry. You're not all here today. And as far as jamming is concerned, you're always all here."

Nothing was a done deal yet. I was still in the middle of writing my college application opus and was still wavering about what to do with my life. But for the first time, when I looked into my future, instead of seeing Johnny, Chey, and Richie, I was seeing a dorm room where I could hang my Ramones poster, a quad where I could sit quietly and play an acoustic guitar under a tree, and a girl who would want to be with me just to be with me.

I know, it's stupid.

It was too soon to share all that with anyone else, so I decided that the status quo would be best.

"No," I told Johnny. "I'm all here, just like always."

"Good," he said. "Because right now this band is the world to me." There was a note of urgency and sincerity, or maybe it was desperation, that underlined every word.

We went back inside to pick up the rehearsal again.

"Harry," Johnny said, "let's do that new song you played for us last week."

He meant "Pleasant Sounds." It made me feel awkward as hell, but what was I supposed to do? Johnny had been working on the keyboard part—a gentle line to counterbalance and punctuate the guitar riff—which, when added to the mix, made the song much more interesting.

When we were running through it for the third time and while I was playing the chorus, which has a couple of major seventh chords, Johnny stopped us and looked at Chey.

"That bass line isn't working."

"Sorry?"

"The bass line," he repeated, a note of exasperation in his voice, "isn't working. The notes are clashing with the chords Harry's playing. You should be landing on the root note."

Chey, who never liked being told what to do and who seemed out of sorts to begin with, folded her arms and rested them on her bass. "And now you're an expert on bass guitars?"

"No," Johnny snapped. "I'm an expert on what sounds good and on the crap that doesn't."

Whoa. While this was definitely a flash of the old Johnny, even the old Johnny would never have told Cheyenne she sounded like crap.

"Sorry," he said, and hung his head. I could see the tension in his jaw. "But do me a favor and try it with a simpler line that focuses on the root notes."

Chey was clearly pissed, but she nodded, said, "Fine," and tried it Johnny's way.

Of course, he was right. The tweak in the bass made the song a thousand times better. But that wasn't the point.

Something was going on with Johnny, and it wasn't good.

"Pleasant Sounds" turned out to be one of our best songs. It was quintessential Scar Boys. But at what cost?

"I talked to Carol at CB's," Johnny said matter-of-factly when we took our next break, "and they can fit us in the second Friday or second Saturday in December."

"Better make it the Saturday," Chey said.

We all looked at her, waiting for more.

"I got a job." She waited for us to react, but honestly, I think we were too stunned. "I'm working Friday nights from now on."

The times, they were a-changin'.

CHEYENNE BELLE

I think I was the first one of the Scar Boys to ever do an honest day's work. But I was motivated. I felt like I had to take control of the few things that were actually in my control, you know? And paying Theresa and Agnes back became a priority. It was also something for me to focus on other than all the horrible stuff I was feeling.

Both girls were home when I was getting ready to go to the mall to look for a job, both of them watching my every move as I got dressed.

"What the hell are you doing?" Theresa asked.

It was only a few days after the D & C, and besides what I was feeling emotionally, I was still hurting physically, so I'd taken my meds. The painkillers the doctor had given me—Vicodin—were making *everything* numb, not just my belly. My feet felt numb, my arms felt numb, my tongue felt numb. Best of all, my brain felt numb. I'd taken one half an hour before I'd started trying on clothes, and I was feeling pretty good.

"I'm going out to look for work," I answered Theresa, my voice something between tired and singsongy, "to pay you guys back. I want to look the part." I was tossing each piece of clothing I owned onto a pile on my bed. Nothing seemed right.

I like to think that my style is my utter lack of style. Most days, I throw on whatever pair of shorts or pants happens to be lying around, and grab whichever T-shirt—washed or not—is within arm's reach. The only time I ever bother to think about my appearance is at gigs. And even then, my approach to fashion is *casual* with a capital *C*.

For a job, I figured it was different.

Problem was, I didn't own any interview clothes. I mean, I had some old Easter outfits that might still fit, but I didn't think that a frilly white dress with white tights and Mary Janes were going to score me a gig at Sam Goody's.

Luckily, Agnes is petite, too, and she came to the rescue. Sort of.

"Try these."

"Really?"

It was a magenta skirt and a cream-colored blouse, with a turquoise blazer that had massive shoulder pads. "Yes, really."

I tried them on. "I look like Jo from *Facts of Life*."

"Better that than looking like a scary punk rock girl."

"I am a scary punk rock girl."

"One, you're not scary, and two, the stores in the mall don't hire scary punk rock girls."

"Not even the record store?"

"It's the mall, Cheyenne."

"What do you think?" I asked Theresa. She had been quiet, and even though I don't think she knew any more about this stuff than I did, I figured a second opinion wouldn't hurt.

"I think Mrs. Garrett is going to love it."

Agnes laughed and I groaned. I don't know why I bothered.

Anyway, I didn't see any other options. I put on the most sensible pair of shoes I owned (the Easter dress Mary Janes), took my bag, checked to make sure I had a pen—someone once told me to always have a pen when you're applying for jobs—and left.

The Cross County Shopping Center isn't really a mall in the way a mall is a mall. For one thing, it's outdoors. There's no enclosed building, no food court, none of the things more modern malls—like the Galleria in White Plains—have. It's just a few intersecting walkways lined with scrubby trees and tacky stores.

It was late afternoon, so all of the high school girls were out shopping. I swear to God, not one of them was taller than five feet, but with their shoes each one was closer to six, especially when you factored in the tower of hair. At least the weather had turned colder, so they were wearing jackets and I didn't have to look at their belly buttons. Between May first and September thirtieth, not one girl in Yonkers ever wore a shirt that covered her belly button. It's like it was a local law or something. I think it was true on Long Island and in New Jersey, too. I don't know why, but belly buttons kind of freak me out. They're weird, you know?

Anyway, my first stop was Sam Goody's. I'd been buying records there for years, so I recognized a lot of the sales staff. Most of them listened to different kinds of music than me—they were more of an arena rock crowd, Journey, Kansas, Starship—but they were usually nice.

I had seen the guy behind the counter a bunch of times. He was tall and thin, with pale skin and hair so blond it was almost white. He looked like a Q-tip.

"Hi," I said.

"Can I help you?"

"I was wondering if you're hiring?"

"Oh, sweetie," the Q-tip said, almost laughing. "This place isn't for you."

"Huh?"

Then, I swear to God, the guy looked me up and down from my head to my toes, taking in the whole package. I felt naked.

And do you know what he said?

"*Facts of Life* doesn't really fit in around here."

I could've killed Agnes.

"Try the bookstore," the Q-tip told me.

So I did.

HARBINGER JONES

Cheyenne's announcement at rehearsal that she had a job caught us off guard. I was too stunned to speak, and Johnny just looked dejected. Wait, strike that. He looked rejected. Like Chey getting a job without his knowledge was a personal affront. Only Richie spoke.

"Fucking A, short stuff. What're you gonna be doing?"

She explained that she was going to be working at the bookstore in Cross County Shopping Center.

I knew that store well.

When I was younger and going through the long and tortured recovery from the lightning strike, books became some of my best friends.

I remember this one day, I was sitting in the science-fiction section reading a Robert Heinlein book, when all of a sudden there was a big commotion coming from the other side of the stacks. I must've been twelve and had convinced my mom it was okay to leave me there while she went shopping at Gimbels.

The bookstore was usually a quiet place, library quiet, so the noise was startling. My first reaction was to shrink and hide, to make myself disappear. The more raucous something was, the more I wanted to avoid being seen. Commotions almost never ended well for me.

But this was a happy noise; I ignored my inner voice and peered around the corner.

A man in priest's clothes stood in the center of a small entourage as the store manager—a guy named Guy—was setting up a table for a book signing. I'd only ever seen a signing here once before, and almost no one came. Already, seven or eight people were on line for this priest.

Only, he wasn't a priest. He was some kind of radio disc jockey who had written an autobiography and was dressing as a priest as a kind of gimmick. I must've stepped all the way out of the science-fiction section without realizing it, because the disc jockey looked straight at me and we locked eyes. For a minute I didn't know which way this was going to go.

"I'd hate to see the other guy," he said. Then his gang—and to me, they'd gone from being an entourage to a gang—turned and looked at me. Their audible gasps were drowned out by their laughter at their boss's incredible wit. I turned on my heel and went back to the books, none of which seemed to want to judge me. I'd been through enough episodes like that in my life to let it wash over me. I picked up the Heinlein book—I think it was *The Moon is a Harsh Mistress*—and started reading again.

A few minutes later, as more and more fans arrived for the signing and the noise from the other side of the bookcases grew, a woman, one of the DJ's gang, poked her head around the corner and found me.

"Hey, kid," she said. I looked up, waiting for the punch

line. "He didn't mean anything by it. That kind of humor is just part of his act."

That kind of humor? I wanted to ask her why people thought it was funny to cut someone else down. Why they thought it was okay to put someone in a situation where they had to defend themselves when there was no possible way of actually doing so. Why cruelty was so fucking hilarious.

But I didn't. I wasn't wired to ask those questions. Besides, I knew the answers. People act like that to make themselves feel superior. People suck.

"So," the woman continued, "he wants you to have this." It was a signed copy of the disc jockey's book. She smiled as she handed it to me. I took it, and she walked away without another word. Part of me wanted to forgive the guy and to embrace and cherish that book. That's what I always did. I made excuses for people, found reasons for their behavior. But this was different; it was a kind of turning point for me. It's the moment where I think I finally got smart enough to be jaded.

I'll bet any amount of money that the priest-disc-jockey douche bag had no idea that woman had given me the signed book. She was doing damage control. I moved a few books on the shelf in front of me and shoved the signed copy all the way to the back. It's probably still sitting there today.

CHEYENNE BELLE

I wasn't the biggest reader in the world, but I did like books. I went through a phase when I was fourteen when I read everything I could by V. C. Andrews. It was horror-romance stuff. You can eat it like candy.

Since then the only things I'd read were the books assigned in my high school English classes and maybe one or two more books during the summer.

Anyway, the bookstore had been at the mall for a long time, and I'd been there before, but I never really paid attention.

Once I started working there, I fell in love with the place—well, parts of it anyway. The corporation that ran the store treated books and employees like hammers and nails. Just like everything else in the grown-up world, businesspeople had found a way to suck the life out of something fun. I mean, how the hell do you suck the life out of books?

But maybe some of that was on me, too. I was in a really crappy place after the miscarriage, and everything in the world seemed a bit off. The hardest part was how completely alone I felt. I used to pride myself on that, on my ability to be alone. For years, I'd been projecting this whole tough-chick image onto the world, and now it was breaking down.

If I had just talked to Johnny or Harry, or even talked

more to Richie, maybe I would've felt better. Instead, I kept my secrets locked up inside, and they were eating me alive. But what was I supposed to do? It's not like my bandmates were rallying around me. Even something as stupid and small as me getting the job at the bookstore caused all this tension—Johnny looked hurt, Harry looked like he didn't care, and Richie just took it in stride. Where were the high-fives? Where were the whoops and hollers and "Way to go, Chey"?

I needed someone or something to hold on to, only there was no one and nothing there.

The pain meds helped when I took them, but they would wear off and the bad feelings would start again. So I started taking them more often.

Dr. McCartney at Planned Parenthood had filled a second prescription of Vicodin a week after the miscarriage. When I asked for a third, she told me I had to come in and see her in person.

This time I made the trip alone. It was a weekday, so the protestors were mostly gone. Only one woman with an oak tag sign that said, *Pray for the souls of the unborn*, stood across the street. She was nice looking, with a plain white blouse and a gray skirt. But she looked angry and confused.

Unlike the phonies and lunatics who had been there on the weekend, I could tell that this lady had lost a baby or had an abortion, and it had messed with her mind. It's like she needed to do something but couldn't figure out what. I guess holding a sign on the side of the road was the best she could think of. I felt sorry for her.

"Cheyenne." Dr. McCartney had half a smile and half a frown when she came into the examination room. "You're still having pain?"

Idiot that I am, I didn't realize that I couldn't get a prescription for pain meds until the end of time just because I wanted one. The pain from the miscarriage was gone. I wanted the meds for everything else. The Vicodin had become the one and only thing that was filling the hole in my life. I don't think I'd really understood that until I was sitting back in the examination room.

I probably waited a whole five seconds before lying.

"Yeah, I am still having pain. Can you give me something?"

"We need to take a look and see what's going on in there," she said, very gently tapping her finger on my belly.

I was nervous. I wanted to run, but I went through with it.

The doctor didn't say a word as she did the ultrasound and did the cervical exam. When she was done, she had me get dressed and meet her in her office. When I sat down she was writing on a pad, and for a second I was pretty psyched. I was going to get the pain meds after all. Only, when she handed me the paper, it wasn't a prescription.

"This is the name of a psychiatrist friend of mine. He can help you with what you're feeling and can help you stop wanting or needing to take the Vicodin."

"I don't need—"

She held up a hand for me to stop. "Cheyenne, I've seen a lot of girls come in here, and I understand what you're going through. But there's nothing physically wrong with you that would require Vicodin."

I slunk out of there with my tail between my legs. I didn't even look at the piece of paper she'd handed me until I was on the bus. I was too embarrassed. When I finally did look, I laughed out loud. It was the phone number for Dr. Kenneth Hirschorn, Harry's shrink, Dr. Kenny. I crumpled it up and shoved it in my pocket. No way was Dr. Kenny the answer to my problems. I didn't want to talk to anyone, least of all Harry's shrink. No, I would just have to find another way.

There was only one person in my life who knew enough creepy people to help me get meds without a prescription, and that was Theresa.

Theresa and I have one thing in common. We're both fearless. I don't mean that we're not afraid of things. We are. It turns out I'm terrified of God and Theresa is scared of spiders. But we're both willing to put ourselves out there, to take chances. Like when I tried out for the Scar

SCAR GIRL

Boys or went on the road with the band. Or like the people Theresa chooses to hang out with.

Her group of friends is pretty loose with drugs and sex and stuff; they're not the kinds of kids you'd bring home to meet Mom and Dad. I think my sister hangs out with them to get attention because she has a self-image problem. She's a really pretty girl, and she's pretty smart; if she would just realize that, maybe she would pick better friends.

Anyway, I thought maybe she could help me get the pain meds. I was wrong. (I'm wrong a lot.)

"You want me to get you what?" It was later that same night, and we were alone in our room.

"Vicodin. I just need them for a little while, to feel better, that's all."

She snorted. "No, Cheyenne. I can't help you get prescription meds. Why don't you just drink, like a normal person?" she said, and she put her headphones back on.

And that's just what I did.

PART FIVE,
EARLY DECEMBER 1986

We're the Oakland A's of rock and roll.
On the field, we can't be beat, but in the
clubhouse, well, that's another story.
—Glenn Frey

Of all the places you've played over the years, what's your favorite venue?

HARBINGER JONES

Without a doubt, it's CBGB's.

RICHIE MCGILL

CB's.

CHEYENNE BELLE

It's not actually a nightclub or an arena. It's the basement in Harry's parents' house. That's where we jammed in the early days of the band. His mom would always have a snack and drinks for us, and we just had fun. It was all about the music and about friendship. It will never get any better than that.

HARBINGER JONES

My dad was home from Albany for all of December. The legislature wasn't in session, and politics tended to quiet down at the holidays. Even though he and I had managed to make a kind of weird peace, the level of stress in my life always grew by leaps and bounds when my dad was in the house. I was about to change all of that.

"I think I want to apply to college." My parents both looked up from their morning newspapers—my dad, the *Times*; my mom, the *Herald Statesman*—like someone'd sat down at the kitchen table and started speaking Chinese. "You know, for real, this time," I added.

A smile stretched from one of my mom's ears to the other, but my father looked suspicious. The whole pretending-to-apply-and-get-accepted-to-college was a dick move on my part, and I didn't blame my dad for harboring some resentment.

"Why?" my father asked. He folded his hands on the table and tried to bore a hole through my face with his eyes.

"I don't know, just feels like it's time."

"And the Scar Boys?"

"Maybe it's time to move on, that's all." Note that I said "maybe." I was still hedging my bets.

He was back to staring me down, trying to find the source of some new lie. He wasn't going to find it, because it wasn't there.

"What do you want to study?"

"I haven't figured that out yet. My understanding is that you don't need to pick a major until your junior year. Maybe something with math or science?" I hadn't really thought about math and science, but it was the one part of high school where I'd shown some aptitude, and he knew that. I was playing to my audience.

"Mm-hmm." He was trying to be tough, but I could see he was buying in. My dad has a tell when you're winning him over: he finally shuts up.

He and I had a strained relationship from the word go, but it changed after I came back from Athens. It took me a while to figure out, but at some deep and secret level, I think my father actually respected me for going on the road with the band. Outwardly, he hated the Scar Boys, hated the music, hated the image, hated how much I'd lied to him, and hated that the band had steered me off the straight and narrow. But he had spent so many years viewing me as this helpless little gimp that when I stood up and did something on my own, I think maybe he was kind of proud.

Since coming back from Georgia, everything about the way my dad treated me was, I don't know, more gentle. Like this one Saturday, when he was home from Albany—his work as a legislative liaison for the governor had him out of the house four nights a week—he came into my room and said, "C'mon, let's go."

"Where are we going?"

"Just grab a jacket. It'll be fun."

Fun? Fun was not a word I associated with my dad, but it was three hours until rehearsal, so I grabbed my jacket and went. After everything I'd put my parents through, I figured I owed them the little things.

Ten minutes later we stepped out of my dad's Chevy Nova and onto a strip mall parking lot on Tuckahoe Road. He nodded to the store in front of us and smiled.

"Anthony's Billiards Club," I read aloud. "We're going to shoot pool?"

And that's just what we did. We spent the next two hours playing eight ball and nine ball, and just shooting the shit. At first, I was so taken off my game that I didn't know how to react. I finally asked the question I had to ask.

"Dad, what are we doing here? What's this about?"

He paused a beat before answering. "Look, Harry, I just . . . you and I . . . maybe it would be nice if we spent a little more time together."

I had no idea where this was coming from, and I trusted it the way a hen trusts a fox, but what else could I do other than go with the flow?

My dad turned out to be a really good pool player—I had only played once or twice—and while he did give me some great pointers, I think he also enjoyed kicking my ass. He's just that competitive. He reminded me of what Johnny was like before the accident. Weird.

When we got home, we went our separate ways. Scenes from that afternoon were swirling in my head as I watched him react to my news about wanting to apply for college.

"I think it's wonderful, Harry," my mom said. "And

we'll support you in any way we can. Isn't that right, Ben?"

My father gave my mom a long look before nodding and turning his attention back to me. "Of course, son," he said, while trying to hold back a smile. "Of course."

We spent the next few minutes talking about the application process—I didn't tell them about my epic application essay—and then we were done.

It felt both really good and really bad that I'd told them. Good that it was off my chest and that I had their support, bad that, all of a sudden, it was real. It was my first moment of buyer's remorse.

But nothing was written in stone. Not yet.

CHEYENNE BELLE

We played a nightclub called the Bitter End.

The place had a very different vibe from CBGB's. Where CB's was in the Bowery, the Bitter End was in the Village. Where CB's was a crap hole, the Bitter End was nice. Where CB's history was all punk—and, yes, I do love punk—the Bitter End had more to it. It made its name as a venue for folk artists like Bob Dylan and Joan Baez, before they were famous. Isn't that cool?

Anyway, by this time the band was really humming, and our following was growing. This was the first show where we were the headline act on a weekend in New York City. That was a big deal.

We were blown away when more than a hundred people turned out. Something magical was starting to happen with the Scar Boys.

It was also the first time I played a gig drunk.

I felt like I was being chased. Not by a person, but by all the things I'd done wrong and all the secrets I was keeping—my pregnancy and my miscarriage, for sure, but even before that, my kiss with Harry in Georgia, and before that, my whole relationship with Johnny. So many secrets, and I felt like I needed to outrun them all. And like I said, I'm not so good at asking for help. While being high or drunk didn't really fix things, it made me care less, made my problems seem further away. Farther away? I can never keep those words straight. Grammar kind of sucks.

I didn't drink a lot—just three beers that a creepy old guy at the bar bought me because I let him hit on me. Even though I was totally skeeved, I didn't flinch when he put his hand on my ass. I'm not sure what a guy like that is thinking, but whatever it is, it's messed up.

Given my size and given that I was still a novice with alcohol, those three beers went right to my head. It didn't help that I drank them fast, back to back to back, mostly so I could get up and get away from the creepy guy. It didn't help that I hadn't eaten dinner. And it definitely didn't help that I downed them right before we went on.

Even with all that, I did pretty good with the bass. The

high of music can do a lot to counteract the low of booze. Adrenaline, meet alcohol. It wasn't my best gig, but it wasn't a disaster, either.

We closed our set with "That's Not My Leg." The girl who caught Johnny's peg leg leaped on stage and jumped around like she'd won a million bucks, and the whole place was going crazy.

So of course they were all screaming for an encore. Johnny talked us into having "Pleasant Sounds" ready, in case we got called back up, which wasn't like us. We always ended with something loud and fast, and "Pleasant Sounds" was a ballad. But it worked. Holy shit, did it work. It worked so well that, for the first time ever, we were called back for a *second* encore.

The soundman and the woman handling the lights were pissed. Unless you're playing Madison Square Garden or the Nassau Coliseum, you don't get two encores; the crew just wanted to go home. But this audience wasn't going to let anyone go anywhere. So the lights stayed low and the mics stayed hot.

Problem is, we had no idea what to play. We hadn't planned for this, and as a general rule—really, Johnny's rule—the Scar Boys was a pretty well-scripted act.

"What do we do?" Richie asked as we stood on the side of the stage, a thunderstorm of claps and hollers making it hard to hear one another.

"I have something," Johnny said. "A song I've been working on."

"Something new?" Harry sounded freaked out. "We can't play something new."

"I don't know, seems like a pretty rock-and-roll thing to do, if you ask me." Johnny knew Harry's weak spot. As soon as Harry thinks he's not being rock-and-roll enough, like there's some giant rock meter measuring his life, he needs to find a way to fix it. Richie nodded.

The adrenaline high of the set was fading, and the aftereffect of the beer was making me a bit loopy.

"So how do we play along?" I asked. I think I might've slurred my words because Johnny looked at me funny.

"It's simple. It's the same riff over and over again. The song is all about the dynamics, about how loud and soft we play the riff. Kind of like 'Heroin' by the Velvet Underground. Harry, give me your guitar." Harry did, and Johnny showed him what really was a very easy riff. "It's that, over and over again. Just follow me for how loud and soft to get. Chey, can you follow?"

I'm guessing Johnny singled me out because he could see that I wasn't quite right. The room was spinning a bit, and I really had no idea what he'd just played, but I nodded anyway.

"Richie," Johnny said, "let us get through the first verse or two, then come in big, okay?"

"Got it."

The crowd had organized itself into a steady, rhythmic clap and chant of "Scar Boys, Scar Boys," and when we walked back onstage, they erupted into a frenzy.

There was one guy—a good-looking older guy—sitting at a table in the front row, who wasn't clapping or chanting or even standing. I didn't remember seeing him there before, so he must've snuck up front during the break between songs. He had a big smile on his face, and when he saw me catch his eye, he nodded.

"Thank you, thank you," Johnny said into the mic, sitting down at the piano as the crowd settled down. "We're going to do something kind of crazy."

A few isolated whoops and hoots.

"We're going to play a song that we've never ever played before. Not that we've never played in public, but that we've never played as a band before. In fact, Harry, Cheyenne, and Richie have never even heard it before." Louder whoops and hollers. "It's a song I've been working on, and I thought, *Let's see what these fine people think of it.* Would that be okay with you?"

The room absolutely exploded into a wall of noise and positive energy. Johnny nodded to Harry, and Harry started playing the riff Johnny showed him. He played it perfectly, which brought a smile to Johnny's face, which was good to see. I mean, it's not that Johnny didn't smile;

it's that lately he hadn't seemed to mean it. This time, he did.

Against the backdrop of Harry playing that lonely guitar riff, Johnny started to sing:

> *I am only what I seem*
> *When I hear my mirror confess*
> *That I live in American dreams*
> *And that's useless.*

> *Cracked cement trains of thought*
> *Going off the tracks.*
> *What's the difference if no one's on board?*
> *It's useless.*

That's where Richie and I came in big, and Johnny, as if he knew what we were going to do, added a beautiful organ line.

But I was off, a hair late with everything. And my bass line was too simple. My fingers weren't able to do any of the stuff they would normally do. It was hard enough to land on the root notes and just follow along. My performance was, what's the word, *uninspired*. Johnny shot me a look that was half annoyed and half concerned, and sang the next verse.

Writers spend hours staring out windows,
Watching it rain minutes,
Yet still never a word written
That's useless.

I'll find the girl who cries in the street,
I'll follow her trail of tears.
When I reach the puddles at her feet,
I'll see her washed-out fears
In a puddle of tears,
Drained over the years.
It's useless.

At this point, Johnny held up his hand to have us dial it back and then slashed the air to tell Richie and me to stop.

We did. And again, I was late.

The only sound was Harry's guitar echoing through the room.

With my head in my hands, confused,
Nothing is what it seems.
And just when I thought nothing had use,
I find the only truth
Is in dreams.

Harry played the riff four more times, each one slower than the one before, until he ended on a bright but sad-sounding E chord.

The room was dead quiet for just long enough to make me wonder if I'd really messed up. Then the audience went nuts. And I mean, seriously nuts! I couldn't hear myself think as we leaped off the stage.

Richie high-fived Harry, me, and Johnny, but when I went to hug Johnny, he looked like he was going to kill me.

"What the fuck was that?" He was yelling at me. Harry and Richie looked as surprised as I did.

"What?" I said in full defender mode. "I've never heard the fucking song before."

"Bullshit."

"What do you mean? I've never heard—"

"That's not what I mean, and you know it." Johnny was as pissed as I'd ever seen him. "You played the whole set high or drunk or something, didn't you?"

I had no response, but I didn't break eye contact with him.

"Maybe you don't need this band, Cheyenne," he said, using my full name, which he almost never did, "but Harry and I do."

Harry looked up like he'd been slapped, like he wanted no part of whatever was happening between me and Johnny, like he didn't want to be dragged into the middle.

"Yeah, I'm the first bass player in the fucking history of fucking rock and roll that had a couple of beers before playing a set. You're out of your mind, John." I always shortened his name to *John* when I was being serious with him.

"However many beers Dee Dee Ramone or Paul Simonon had before a set, they never messed up the music."

"I'd never heard the fucking song before!" Now I was shouting.

"Fuck you, Cheyenne." He may as well have punched me in the stomach. *Fuck you, Cheyenne?* For this?

"Whatever," I mumbled, and I walked off to the bathroom.

But even with that big scene, it wasn't the awful thing he'd said that was echoing in my ears as I stomped away. It was his new song.

"Useless." I couldn't get it out of my head.

HARBINGER JONES

The truth is, I'd heard "Useless" before. Johnny had played the song for me a few days earlier, and we'd even worked on it a little bit. I nailed the guitar part at the Bitter End because I'd already played it. That's something I've never told Cheyenne and Richie.

I didn't know why Johnny was making it seem like I'd never heard it, but I figured he had a reason, so I played along.

I asked him about it later.

"Did you know," he answered, "that when Alfred Hitchcock filmed the shower scene in *Psycho*, he used warm water for all the rehearsals? But when it came time for the actual take, he used cold water, only he didn't tell Janet Leigh."

"Who?" I asked.

"She's the woman who gets stabbed in the shower."

"Oh." I'd never seen *Psycho* before, but I knew better than to interrupt Johnny when he got going on something.

"So when they started filming and they needed her to scream, they doused her with the ice-cold water and she gave the performance of her life."

"John," I said, both exasperated and confused, "what does that have to do with 'Useless'?"

He rolled his eyes like I was the biggest idiot in the world for not following his train of thought. "I figured that, if the other guys thought it was a totally new song, it would give the band extra focus."

Johnny was like that. Always looking for a way to push us harder, make us better. He was like our own David Lee Roth. It drove the three of us crazy sometimes, but for the most part, it worked. Whether or not it was his *Psycho* stunt—pun intentional—or something else, "Useless" worked that night, it really did. It was a totally magic moment. At least I thought so.

Only, as soon as we walked offstage, Johnny bit Chey's

head off, accusing her of playing drunk. She had been a little off during the set, but I wasn't really sure where his level of anger was coming from. It ruined the whole good vibe we had going.

I started coiling my guitar cords and packing up my effects pedals in silence while Richie took apart his drum gear. Johnny, who looked really tired, was leaning against the wall; his blond curls, which he was growing out like Roger Daltrey, were matted against a concert poster for when Peter Frampton had played the club. Chey had stormed off to the bathroom.

"You kids were amazing," this guy said as he walked up to us. I'm not sure why older people like to call younger people *kids*. Do they think it endears them to us? It doesn't. It's condescending. You don't need to remind us that you're older, wiser, and in control. We know that every waking minute of every day. It was especially aggravating on that night, because, really, *we* were supposed to be in control.

"Thanks," Richie said. "Who the fuck are you?"

"I'm your fucking future," the guy said. I liked his answer. It made me forget about the *kids* thing for a minute.

"You mean," Richie responded, "like, you're Johnny, but from the future?" He cackled at his own moronic joke, and I went back to coiling my guitar cords while the guy talked.

"Not quite. I manage rock bands, and I'd like to get the

Scar Boys into the studio to cut a demo. I think you guys have something here, and I'd like to get a closer look."

We all stopped what we were doing. He had our full attention now. He was a scrawny man with a big nose and yellow teeth, but also with a certain kind of charisma. He was holding business cards, fanned like a hand of poker.

"Jeff Evans," he said, by way of introduction. We each shook his hand and took a card.

Jeff, seeing how completely dumbfounded we were, just stood there, taking it all in, grinning like he knew something we didn't. Like he knew a lot of things that we didn't.

RICHIE MCGILL

Jeff tried to come on all strong, like he was this wise older dude and we were just a bunch of dumb young punks.

He told us that he managed bands and gave us this whole song and dance about how he was gonna get us to the big time. I was still coming down off the high of the set, and I didn't really know what to make of the dude. At first it sounded like a lot of bullshit.

"So listen up, Scar Boys and Scar Girl," he said, nodding to Chey, who had just walked back up from taking a leak—wait, do girls say *taking a leak*? Anyways, Jeff said, "You're doing great on your own. But you're good enough for bigger venues. I saw you a couple of weeks ago at CBGB's, when you opened for Chemicals Made of Mud. You shouldn't be opening for wankers like that." Jeff loved to say shit like *wanker, tosser,* and *punter.* He was one of those dudes who thought it was cooler to be British than American. I guess when he was younger the cooler bands and better music were coming out of the UK. That's not true anymore. The crap coming out of London in the last few years flat-out sucks. I mean, Kajagoogoo? "If you're going to be an opening act, then you should open for bands playing theaters and small arenas."

"Arenas?" Johnny asked.

"Yes, arenas. Look, I have your single, 'The Girl Next Door.' It's great. The raw emotion on it sucks you right in. But it needs a bit more of a professional touch."

"You mean, make us slick." It was Johnny again. I don't know if he didn't trust Jeff or if he was just still pissed at Chey and acting all cranky because of it.

"No, no. Not slick. But the EQ on the snare drum isn't crisp enough. The whole mix has too much treble. And while I love the stereo tambourine"—I saw Johnny look at Harry and smile at that one—"your records can't live on whimsy alone."

"So how does this work?" Johnny asked.

"Simple. You sign a contract with me, and I work to promote you, to get you better gigs, and to get you a record deal. No money up front, but I keep fifteen percent of whatever you earn."

He said it was simple, but that's one thing I've learned about life: nothing, not one freaking thing, is ever simple.

CHEYENNE BELLE

The next day, we were sitting in a diner in Yonkers. It was a weird place because the building next door was . . . wait for it . . . a diner!

Two diners right next door to each other. I mean, really, what's the point? They were owned by two brothers who supposedly hated each other. After the first guy opened the Olympic Diner, his brother, just to spite him, opened the Five Star Diner thirty yards away. No one knows why they hated each other so much, but I'll bet one of them slept with the other one's wife.

Want to know the weirdest thing of all? Both diners thrived. The parking lots were always jammed, and the booths were always packed. Go figure. I guess people in Yonkers like their diners.

Anyway, we were sitting at a booth in the Five Star, all of us staring at Jeff's card, which Johnny had dropped in the middle of the table.

Johnny hadn't apologized for bitching me out, and I hadn't apologized for playing the gig drunk, but when Harry picked us both up, we seemed to settle into a kind of truce. Jeff's card, and everything it stood for, seemed to be more important than all of that other stuff. Harry said it was like the "one ring to rule them all." He was always geeking out that way.

"What do you guys think?" Johnny said, nodding at the business card. He was always the first to talk. Even after everything that'd happened on the road, even after his accident, even as he was retreating deeper and deeper into his shell and Harry started coming out of his own, Johnny was still the leader of the Scar Boys. At the end of the day, we were going to think whatever he wanted us to think. It's just how we were wired. I'm not saying it was right or wrong; it was just the truth.

"Tell me again what he wants us to do?" I asked. After I had stomped off to the bathroom and then stomped back out, I saw Jeff talking to the band. I walked over in the middle of his spiel, just in time to hear him refer to me as *Scar Girl*. I liked that, a lot.

Johnny went through the whole thing again, laying out all the pros and cons. I asked a few questions but was barely listening. This was a no-brainer to me. Why wouldn't we say yes? Wasn't this everything we'd been working for? I could tell that Richie was thinking the same as me, but Johnny, and especially Harry, seemed, I don't know, hesitant. I didn't get it.

HARBINGER JONES

I looked out the window of the diner and watched the traffic snake along Central Avenue, the main drag that runs through Yonkers and the southern part of Westchester County. The road was like an artery clogged with fat, slowing the entire city down, waiting for it to have a heart attack and die.

I watched all those people in all those cars, wondering where they were going, wondering what they were thinking. It's overwhelming, sometimes, to think about all the people in the world living their lives. What are they feeling? What skeletons are in their closets? Are they leading happy, normal, well-adjusted lives? Or are they drowning in swirling cesspools of drama, just like the rest of us?

I was torn apart looking at Jeff's card. I had more or less made up my mind to leave the band and was just biding my time until the moment was right. But this, this was everything we'd been working toward.

My brain instinctively reached for one of its lists, but it just wasn't there.

I looked at each of my bandmates while Johnny spoke.

Richie, like always, was relaxed, his long and lanky arm up on the back of the booth, like he had it draped across the shoulders of an invisible girlfriend, his free hand holding a Cherry Coke. He was listening to Johnny intently.

Johnny was lost in his own soliloquy. I was only catching every few words—"don't really know this guy"—and "could be the opportunity of a lifetime"—and "I don't know about you guys, but I kind of need this." That last one caught my ear. Johnny never needed anything. Wait, strike that. Johnny never admitted to needing anything. His eyes were glassy, and there was a note of desperation in his voice. He was slowly becoming someone different. It's almost like he was becoming me.

Chey had her full attention on the cup of coffee, now turning cold, on the table in front of her. I could tell she was listening to Johnny because she was asking questions and nodding at appropriate moments, but there was something underneath.

I was pretty surprised that Chey had gotten drunk at the Bitter End—not that she was a total prude—but like it is for me, music is Cheyenne's everything, and I'd never seen her do anything to put that in jeopardy. Johnny was kind of a dick the way he treated her about playing drunk, but he wasn't entirely wrong.

Either way, I was sick of the drama, sick of all the crap running under the surface. The Scar Boys had become like a giant septic tank.

(*Giant Septic Tank*, by the way, is a great name for a band.)

I looked from Johnny, Richie, and Chey back to the

cars on Central Avenue. All those people living all those complicated, mysterious, uncertain lives out there, my best friends in here, and I wasn't sure I knew one group any better than the other. It made me wonder if you can ever really get to know someone.

"So," Johnny said, wrapping up, "I vote that we sign, but maybe only for six months. If this guy turns out to be a bust, then at least we can have a quick out. This is a big decision, so let's vote. Richie?"

"I'm in."

"Chey?"

"Me, too."

"Harry?"

And there it was, my conundrum.

Was I supposed to tell them that I'd been planning to move on, to give them a chance to replace me in the band, or to maybe rethink their decision? Or was I supposed to abandon the notion of college and refocus my energy and my industry on the only dream I'd ever really had, especially now that it had a better chance of coming true, even if that meant having to deal with the Johnny and Cheyenne Show, in all likelihood, ratcheted up to another level?

My brain was still telling me to leave the Scar Boys, my dad's voice—"It's a million-to-one shot that your band can ever make it big"—floating in the air around me. But I still couldn't bring myself to quit.

See? Once a coward, always a coward. I would go along with it for now and figure it all out when the time was right.

I signed.

PART SIX,
LATE DECEMBER 1986

I used to jog, but the ice cubes kept falling out of my glass.
—David Lee Roth

Choose one word to define each of your bandmates.

CHEYENNE BELLE

For Richie, that's easy; I'd say *rhythm*. For Harry, I don't know. It's a lot harder because he's a more complicated guy. Oh, wait, there you go. I'd say *complicated*.

HARBINGER JONES

One word? I think we've already established that I don't do well with word counts, and one word is like the mother of all word counts. That said, for Cheyenne it would have to be *magical*, and for Richie, *true friend*.

Yes, that's two words. Deal with it.

RICHIE MCGILL

One word for Cheyenne? *Feisty*, I guess.

For Harry, that's a snap. *Harbinger*. I didn't even know that was a word other than his name until I'd known him for, like, two years, but, holy shit, it fits. Whether his parents just got it right or whether it forced him to be who he is, I have no idea. But, man, that name fits the dude to a T.

CHEYENNE BELLE

The next couple of weeks passed in a blur.

The mental scars from the miscarriage weren't healing. I kept seeing that baby's face, a little, miniature Johnny, its eyes always closed, like it was sleeping. I lived in terror that it would wake up and start talking to me.

I started drinking more and more to keep the image away. The more time I spent out of it, the less time I had to think about everything that'd happened.

Hold on, that's not really right. It's not like I was drinking and doing other stuff because I knew it would make things better. It was more the other way; that being drunk was the only feeling I liked, or maybe not *liked*, but that I could deal with.

Thanks to my dad, my house was like a training ground for budding alcoholics. A local liquor store, Mallas Wines and Spirits, delivered a quart of Christian Brothers brandy twice a week. I wonder why they call liquor spirits? Maybe because when you're drunk all the time you fade away a little, turning into a kind of ghost.

Anyway, it was easy to sneak shots when my dad fell asleep (by which I mean passed out) on the La-Z-Boy. When the bottles started emptying sooner than they used to, he just figured he was drinking more and ordered his brandy more often. And like I said, my mother had a blind spot when it came to my father's drinking, so she didn't say a word when the kid from the liquor store started coming three times a week.

I spent a lot of that holiday season fucked up, and no one knew. I got really good at hiding it.

Johnny had called and invited me to Christmas dinner at his house. Even though rehearsals were going well, he still hadn't apologized for the whole "fuck you" thing, and we still weren't really talking outside of the band. I think the dinner invitation was him extending an olive branch. While I think I was ready for us to try to get back together, I really didn't like his parents, and the thought of spending Christmas with them wasn't my idea of fun. Besides, just like we did every year, the Belle family was going to Rockland County to my aunt Kathy's house—my dad's sister—for Christmas dinner. I loved my aunt and really wanted to see her.

Kathy was three years younger than my dad and was beautiful, glamorous, and really cool. She was on her second marriage and third career. She'd just finished nursing school and had landed a job in the neonatal unit at the Westchester Medical Center, and was in an even more festive mood than usual when we got to her house.

"Cheyenne!" She wrapped me in a big hug as soon as I walked into the living room. Then she stopped suddenly, held me away at arm's length, her hands gripping my shoulders like a vise, and stared into my eyes. "We'll talk later," she said, and then turned to greet each of my sisters.

Dinner was good. Kathy's latest husband, Greg, was some kind of expert cook. He made a glazed ham, glazed carrots, and glazed onions—I guess he liked glaze—and they were all delicious. My mom made the dessert, a chocolate cake.

"This is wonderful, Susan," Aunt Kathy said to my mother. It took all my mom's effort to grunt a thank-you. My mom hated my aunt Kathy. She used to tell us girls not to turn out like our aunt, that she had no moral compass, no love or respect for Jesus and God.

The truth is, I think my mom was jealous of her sister-in-law. Jealous that she had the nerve to leave an unhappy marriage, jealous that she had the courage to chase her dreams, and jealous that, unlike my mom, Aunt Kathy celebrated, rather than hid, her beauty.

After dinner, when Agnes, Joan, and I were washing and drying dishes, Aunt Kathy tapped me on the shoulder and told me to come with her. I put down the dish towel and followed her down the hall and into her bedroom.

She kicked her shoes off, hopped up on the bed, and sat down cross-legged. She patted the spot next to her, so I followed suit.

"So," she said, taking my hands and looking straight into my eyes, "how long has this been going on?"

I played dumb. "How long has what been going on?"

Aunt Kathy rolled her eyes. "Cheyenne, I'm not a narc, and I'm not a prude, and I won't tell your parents, but maybe I can help you."

All I had to do was let myself go and tell Aunt Kathy everything that had happened, everything that was happening. Part of me knew that if I got it off my chest it would all be okay.

"Chey?"

. . .

I couldn't do it.

I couldn't do it because I was ashamed. Ashamed of what I'd done and ashamed of the lies I'd told. I loved Aunt Kathy and looked up to her. I was sure that, if I told her, she would never love me the same way again. That, by the way, might be the dumbest thought I've ever had in my entire life, which has been a life filled with nothing but dumb thoughts.

And, yeah, I'm not good at asking for help.

"There's nothing going on," I said. "I'm fine."

She looked at me like she was weighing her options. In the end, she did what she thought was right.

"Okay, sweetie," she said. I loved that she called me and my sisters sweetie and honey and sugarplum. "Just know that I'm here if you need me. I can get to Yonkers in a flash. You have my phone number, right?"

I nodded, feeling like I was going to cry. "Let me write

it down anyway." She did, and I stuck the piece of paper in my pocket. "Do you want a minute by yourself? You can stay in here if you do."

I said I did, so she hugged me and left.

I sat on her bed for a while, too numb to actually cry, which made it worse. Then I noticed a small flask on the top of my aunt's dresser. I opened it and took a whiff.

Yep. Alcohol. You gotta love my family.

I took three long sips and rejoined the party.

HARBINGER JONES

Johnny called me on Christmas Day.

That by itself wasn't weird. We'd spent a bunch of holidays together since we first became friends in middle school. Every Halloween and Fourth of July, but also a bunch of Thanksgivings and Christmases, almost always at my house, as his mother seemed to think of me as the village idiot. Or at least she used to.

When Johnny called, my parents and I were getting ready to leave for my grandmother's house in Stamford—she had moved there when my grandfather died, to be closer to Uncle Jamie, my mom's only brother.

Uncle Jamie never got married and never had any kids, and he had all kinds of mental problems. I guess my grandmother moved there thinking she could take care of him. We had no idea if he would even show up for

Christmas dinner, and in some ways, I think my mom was hoping he wouldn't. In the dictionary next to the entry for *black sheep*, there's a picture of my uncle Jamie.

"Hey," Johnny said when I picked up the phone. "Merry Christmas."

"Yeah," I said. "You, too."

I'd been keeping my distance from Johnny and Chey, and even though I had no reason to, from Richie, too. Guilt by association, I guess. I was still sorting out what to do with my future, still writing my now book-length college essay, and just enjoying my time alone.

That's actually kind of funny, when I think about it today. All I wanted as a kid was to be with other people. But then, after everything that had happened with the Scar Boys, I found myself craving space.

"How was the annual haul at Casa de Jones?" he asked. It was a well-known fact that my parents—strike that, it was a well-known fact that my *mother* liked to spoil me rotten, and Christmas was her Super Bowl. Nineteen eighty-six was no different. Aside from the plethora of guitar gear— strings, patch cords, this reverb pedal I'd had my eye on— she got me a whole bunch of stuff meant for a college dorm room. I'd only told my parents about my plans to apply a couple of weeks before Christmas, but already under the tree were two comforters (why I needed two, I couldn't figure out) with sheets and pillowcases, a desk blotter, a bulletin board, and, get this, an actual desktop computer.

I'd used computers in the lab at school and once at Johnny's house (his dad's), but we'd never had one at home. I'd already set it up, planning to play with it that night when I got home from my grandmother's.

But rather than tell Johnny about all the loot, I just gave a vague answer. "You know, the usual embarrassment of riches. You?"

"The same," he said. "So listen." It was his serious-Johnny voice. "I'm worried." I expected him to say he was worried about me, about how distant I'd been. "I'm worried about Chey."

"Chey? What about Chey?" My brain was trying to catch up.

He was quiet.

"John, if this is about that night at the Bitter End, you need to let it go. It was a one-time thing."

"It's more than that. She's been really distant lately, like she's pushing me away." I'd been so busy pushing the two of them away that I hadn't noticed. Or maybe I had but was deliberately not paying attention. "Has she talked to you?" Johnny's voice cracked on the last *you*. "I mean, you and Chey seem pretty close. She seemed to really connect with 'Pleasant Sounds.'"

And there we were, to the heart of the matter. Johnny McKenna, the once great and mighty Johnny McKenna, was actually jealous of me, and not just jealous of me, but jealous of me and Chey. I would be a big fat liar to suggest that some small and thoroughly unlikable part of me didn't smile on the inside.

"No, Johnny," I said softly, but as firmly as I could. "I haven't seen Chey outside of the band since that day I first played 'Pleasant Sounds' at your house." Then I thought for a second and added, "I've been taking a breather from everything."

He let out a big breath of air. "Okay, Harry, thanks," he said, ignoring the opening I was giving him to *really* talk. I think by that point, Johnny was starting to check out of reality.

"Dude, why don't you just call her and talk to her?"

"I tried to invite her for Christmas dinner, but she made up some story about having to go to her aunt's house."

"Did you stop to think that maybe she really did have to go to her aunt's house?"

Silence.

"Call her, John. Remember what happened last time you shut her out?"

"Yeah," he said after a minute. "I guess you're right."

"If you would just start with that presumption, the world would be a better place."

"Huh?"

"Start with the presumption that I'm right. That if

I'm right, the world would be a better place. It's a joke."

Finally, I heard a chuckle. "Asshole." That was the old Johnny. "Tell your parents I said Merry Christmas, too," he said, meaning to end the call. "Wait," I said.

Silence.

There was something stopping me from hanging up. Like a feather tickling my brain, and not in a good way.

"Listen," I started, but I didn't know how to finish. At this point in the conversation Johnny would normally jump in and seize control, but not today. "I'm sorry if I've been a bit, I don't know, distant. Like you said at rehearsal, maybe I haven't been all here."

"Is everything okay?" He sounded genuinely concerned. Like he really wanted to help me. Like he felt bad for not asking. That's the kind of friend he was.

"Yeah," I said. "I've just been taking some time to clear my head. It's been a crazy year." There was a pause, and then I realized it had been a much worse year for him. "I mean not as crazy as your year, but still kind of crazy."

"It's okay, Harry. I understand."

"Anyway, I just didn't want you to get the wrong idea."

There was a sigh on the other end of the phone. I couldn't read between the lines of that sigh. Was Johnny exasperated with me? Was he as tired of my bullshit as I was of his? Or was he just tired, and sad?

"Anyway, like I said," he started again, "tell your folks I

say Merry Christmas."

"Yeah, man, I know they'd wish you the same."

CHEYENNE BELLE

I figured Johnny was pissed at me for blowing him off for Christmas dinner, and I wasn't even sure we were still going out—we hadn't had a private moment since the Bitter End gig—so I was surprised he called me the next day.

I was in my room, enjoying my one and only Christmas present, a Rubik's Cube from my youngest sister, Katherine. With so many Belle girls to deal with, instead of everyone doling out presents to everyone else, our family held a Christmas grab bag. Each December first, while we were putting up our fake Christmas tree with the garland and decorations already on it (and, of course, our nativity scene, because God knows you can't have Christmas without a really tacky nativity scene), we would each pull the name of one family member out of a hat. For a while it was just the seven sisters, but since last year, even my parents threw their names in. They still bought presents for the three kids under twelve, but for the rest of us it was the luck of the draw.

I got Agnes. She's easy to shop for; just find something sensible. I got her a set of very nice colored pens. They were what the bookstore called sidelines, and I got them at a big discount. She seemed to really like them. As for my

Rubik's Cube, for a present from a seven-year-old, it was pretty good. And, hey, it's the thought that counts.

Anyway, I was getting pretty wrapped up in trying to make the damn thing work but could never get more than one side at a time to match colors. I wanted to give it to Harry to see how he would do with it. I also wanted to smash it with a hammer. Anyway, that's what I was doing when the phone rang. A minute later, my mother was calling up to me.

"Cheyenne, there's a boy on the phone!" She underlined the word *boy*. I hated that she did that. She had to announce to the whole universe that a boy was calling me, like she was trying to shine a light on my future life of sin. If she'd only known.

Plus, it's not like she didn't know Johnny, Harry, and Richie, the only boys who would ever actually call me. I mean, it'd been forever since any other boy had called me. I think the last one must've been Greasy Jack.

That was the name my family gave him. And he didn't call on the phone; he was dumb enough to show up at the door.

Jack went to St. Augustine, an all-boys Catholic school that was somehow connected to Our Lady of the Perpetual Adoration. I met him at a birthday party—I didn't really have friends, so I was there as a pity invite—and he just kept hanging around me. I tried to stand quietly in the corner until it was time for my mom to pick me up, but he wouldn't leave me alone.

"Do you like sports?" and "What kind of music do you listen to?" and "What's your favorite TV show?" and "Are you going to the freshman mixer?"

That last one caught my attention.

"What freshman mixer?"

He told me that twice a year our two schools held a joint mixer. It's one of those rituals that cheesy movies seem to get right. Boys stand on one side of a badly lit and badly decorated gym, while girls stand on the other. The popular kids spend the night trying to sneak shots of alcohol.

"At your school, in November," he said. "Are you going?"

"I didn't even know about it."

"Well, now you do."

The guy was pushy as hell, but he was cute in a goofy kind of way, too. He had a mop of light brown hair that matched his eyes. I liked that he wore a Clash pin on his denim jacket.

"What's your name?"

"Jack."

"I don't think I'm really allowed to go on dates, Jack," I told him. I didn't know if this was true, because I'd never been asked on a date before. I wasn't even really sure I was being asked.

"Well, if we meet at the dance, it's not really a date, is it?"

"I guess."

So I went to the mixer—my mother approved of any school-sanctioned event—and met up with Jack. We danced and then snuck outside and kissed. He was the first boy I'd ever kissed, which was a big deal for about one minute, but then the novelty wore off. He had braces, and his breath smelled like pepperoni.

I thought that was that until two days later when he showed up on my front step. I was in the living room, sitting next to my dad, trying to hear a *M*A*S*H* rerun over his snoring, when the doorbell rang. "I'll get it," I called. My mother got there first.

"Hi, is Cheyenne at home?" Jack was wearing the same denim jacket, this time with more buttons, including one that said *Sex Pistols* and one that said *I'd Kill Flipper for a Tuna Sandwich*. His hair was slicked back with some kind of goop, though in God's name I couldn't tell you why. I guess he thought it made him look more presentable. I thought it made him look more like a serial killer. By this time, three of my sisters and I were standing behind my mom.

"Oh, hey, Chey," he said, craning his neck around my mom to see me. "Do you want to go for a walk?"

"No," my mother said before I could answer, her voice all serious and mean. "Cheyenne does not want to go for a walk with a boy that has a sex button on his jacket. Come back wearing nicer clothes, and perhaps I'll introduce you to her father so you can ask permission properly.

"And get a haircut," she added as she closed the door in Jack's face.

My sisters howled with laughter. I wanted to die. "Mom!"

She didn't say anything, just walked by me with her head held high, like she'd won some sort of morality contest. I was fourteen, for Christ's sake.

Anyway, from that day on, my sisters and mother referred to him as *Greasy Jack*.

For the record, he never came back, and I never went looking for him.

HARBINGER JONES

Greasy Jack? Yeah, I've heard the story of Greasy Jack.

I actually knew Jack. My mother and his mother were in the same bowling league, and he was forced to have playdates with me when we were younger.

When he found out I was in a band with Cheyenne Belle, he called and asked me all sorts of questions about her. This was like two years after the two of them'd met. I'd already heard the story from Chey, so I turned the tables and asked him about it. According to Jack, he and Chey did kiss at the mixer, but when he called her house several times over the next several days, she wouldn't come to the phone. Mrs. Belle, according to Jack, was never anything but pleasant. Jack never showed up at her door.

But that's Chey. It's a better story her way, even if the truth is stretched a little bit.

CHEYENNE BELLE

When my mom said there was a boy on the phone, I rolled my eyes and picked up the receiver that sat between my bed and Theresa's. My sister lived her life on that thing, so I hardly ever used it. If some girl from school wasn't calling her to gossip, then some boy was calling to flirt.

It was Johnny.

"Hey, Chey," he said, in response to my weak "Hello?"

"Hey."

"How was Christmas at your aunt's house?"

"It was good." That was a lie, and Johnny probably knew it. "How was dinner at your house? Sorry again I couldn't make it." That was a lie, too.

"It was nice. Just me and my parents." He sounded, I don't know, sad, and there was a brief pause in the conversation.

"Did you get any good presents?" I asked. He had just the one brother, Russell, who didn't live at home, so Johnny was pretty spoiled, though I don't really think he acted spoiled. Since this was the first Christmas after losing his leg, the haul of presents was even bigger than normal.

He rattled off this incredible amount of loot he'd found under the Christmas tree while I listened. It's amazing how two people can talk about so much while talking about absolutely nothing. It was like everything between us was so damaged that neither one of us could talk about it. It was early in the day, and I was feeling jittery. That's not quite right. I was *feeling* . . . period. I didn't want to *feel* anything. I wanted to cut the call short.

Johnny finished itemizing his list of Christmas presents, which trailed off into another long pause. He didn't ask what I got because he knew it would just be embarrassing for both of us.

"Chey," he started, "we need to talk." *Chey, we need to talk.* That's never, ever a good thing. It's pretty much the exact phrase every boy uses before he breaks up with you.

"What about?" I asked. My whole body now felt like a sore tooth that needed Anbesol.

"I don't know, all kinds of stuff. Can we get together before rehearsal tomorrow?"

"Isn't Richie picking us both up?"

"Yeah, well, maybe we could meet somewhere first. Can you come over here?"

I don't know why that pissed me off. It shouldn't have pissed me off. I mean, the guy was walking around on a fake leg, right? But it was always me going to his house. Never him coming to my house, or even my neighborhood.

When I think about it now, I was probably mad because of that day I'd walked all the way to his house when I was pregnant and feeling like shit, the day before I lost the baby. And even though I know it's not true, some part of me feels like the long walk up and down that hill caused my miscarriage.

"Can't we just talk at rehearsal?" I asked.

"I want us to be alone."

"So we'll go outside and talk."

Johnny was quiet for a long moment. "Yeah, okay." He sounded for all the world like he'd just lost something important. He regrouped and started again, this time somehow managing to sound more serious.

"Cheyenne, listen—"

"Give it *back!*" My sister Patricia, nine years old, ran into the room ahead of my sister Joan, ten years old. Their birthdays are ten and a half months apart, what some people called Catholic twins. Patricia was holding Joan's diary, her Christmas grab-bag present from Agnes (also bought with my store discount), in the air, high over her head.

Even though Joan was older, she let Patricia push her buttons every time. (Patricia was actually kind of a bully.)

"Chey, make her give it back!"

"John," I said, using his more serious name, "I have to go. I'll see you tomorrow." And I hung up.

Saved by the Belle. That's a joke we use a lot in our house, and this time it felt real.

I separated my sisters, then hung out in the living room, waiting for my father to fall asleep so I could sneak some of his brandy.

HARBINGER JONES

Our first rehearsal after Christmas was just awkward.

Richie had borrowed his dad's car and picked up Johnny and Chey. I was in my parents' basement, sitting on my amp, messing around on the guitar, when they came in.

Johnny and Chey were both tight-lipped. That's really the only word to describe how they looked; their mouths were straight lines pulled taut across their faces. Richie, who trailed them into the room, looked at me and rolled his eyes.

I mumbled hello, not wanting to get caught in the crosshairs of whatever was going on, and turned my attention to Richie.

"How was Christmas?"

"You're never going to believe it," he said. "The old geezer got me a bike." *Old geezer* sounds like Richie hated his dad, but really it's a term of affection, though not one his father was at all aware existed.

"A bike?"

"Yeah, dude, a bike! It's used, but it kicks ass. It's a 1973 Honda 450cc road bike, and it runs great. My dad and I spent yesterday taking apart the engine and putting it back together. It was awesome. "

"Did you ride it here?" I was excited. I'd never been on a motorcycle before. "Is it outside?"

"Dude, it's winter. And, dude"—Richie was in his *dude* phase then—"I had to pick up these mopes," he said, pointing at Johnny and Cheyenne.

Neither one was paying any attention to our conversation. Chey had her head down, tuning her bass to an electric tuner, and Johnny was sitting behind the keyboard, playing something with the volume low.

"Right," I said to Richie. "But when the weather warms up, I want a ride."

"Definitely," he answered.

Sensing a lull in the conversation, Cheyenne, without warning, launched into one of the few songs in our set that starts with the bass guitar. It was "Girl in the Band." It's an unwritten rule that when one of us starts playing, everyone else jumps on board. So we did. We tore through that song at what felt like twice the normal speed and then just kept playing songs, one after the other—it was kind of like chain-smoking—until an hour had gone by and we were all exhausted. It was pretty incredible.

The mood in the room had softened in the warm glow of good music. That feeling was, unfortunately, short-lived.

"Chey, can I talk to you outside for a minute?"

All three of us looked at Johnny; then Richie and I looked at Chey.

She nodded. They left.

"Did they have a fight or something on the ride over?" I asked Richie after they walked out. I don't know why I asked; I felt so done with the whole thing. I guess I was like a junkie who couldn't live without his fix.

"No, dude. Neither one of them said a word. It was like Superman's secret fortress. Fro-zen."

CHEYENNE BELLE

It was cold in Harry's backyard. Witch's tit cold. I didn't have a jacket on, so I hugged my arms around my chest.

"Chey," Johnny started. "I—" And he stopped. "I—" he started again, but didn't get any further the second time.

For all the world, Johnny looked like he was going to cry again.

I had snifted some of my dad's brandy before I left the house—snifting is how you drink brandy, did you know that?—and I had a nice little buzz going. I wasn't drunk, but I wasn't 100 percent in the moment, you know? I was also a little paranoid. I thought Johnny was going to come after me again for drinking, and I wondered if he could smell it on me. I was chewing gum all the time then, and I'd started wearing perfume to cover the smell, but I was freaked out just the same.

"Chey," he started again.

"C'mon, Johnny, it's freezing out here. What is it?" My tone of voice was pure bitch. I sounded like Theresa.

"It's just that—" He stopped again, and now I was getting mad.

"Jesus Christ, will you just spit it out already?" And then it all came spewing out of me. It was like throwing up on Harry, but so much worse. That was only puke. Disgusting, but harmless. This was daggers, arrows, and bullets. "What is it? Are you going to yell at me for drinking again? Are you going to prove once and for all how uptight you really are? Am I playing the bass wrong again? Am I just not good enough for you? Will I ever be good enough for you? What. The fuck. Is it?!"

I'm sure Johnny thought I was still mad about our blowup at the Bitter End. But I knew the truth. This was about the pregnancy.

I know, I know. It doesn't make any sense. Johnny didn't know I had carried and lost his baby, our baby. He was in the dark, and that wasn't his fault. I can't defend or explain the way I acted. It's just the way it was, you know?

I was letting myself fall deeper and deeper into this big fat hole I'd been digging, and pretty soon there wasn't going to be any way to climb back out. Worst of all, I was pushing Johnny further away.

Anyway, he let out a heavy sigh, something he'd been doing more of lately, looked at the ground, and said, "Nothing. Never mind."

"Whatever," I mumbled, and started to head back inside.

"Wait." This time, Johnny's voice was decisive. "Here." He thrust a small wrapped gift in my hands. He said, "Merry Christmas," and went back into Harry's basement.

HARBINGER JONES

I don't know what they talked about outside, but Johnny came back in first and said he wasn't feeling well and wanted to clear his head. "I'm going to walk home," he told us. It was only about a ten-minute walk, but with Johnny's leg and all, I was surprised.

"You sure you don't want a ride?" Richie asked.

"No, I really need the fresh air." He was already walking up the stairs before I could say anything.

Part of me thought the guy really did need to clear his head. But another part wondered if I should go after him, ask him what had happened with Chey, and I almost did.

I could feel the words start to form in my mouth: *Johnny, wait.* But there was no breath to push them out. I just didn't have any more air in my lungs for this. It was a sin of omission, and it was an act of either exhaustion or cowardice. I plead guilty to both.

When Chey came back inside a minute later, she was pale like the December sky. I thought she might throw up on me again. Instead, she asked Richie to take her home, and he did.

CHEYENNE BELLE

I waited 'til I was alone in the bathroom at my house before opening the present Johnny had given me. It was a small, gold, engraved pick. It said in tiny type, *For Cheyenne, my rhythm and melody, Merry Christmas, Johnny.*

I wanted to die.

PART SEVEN,
JANUARY 1987

No one wants to be the one to say the party's over.
—John Lennon

What do you miss most about home when you're on the road?

HARBINGER JONES

Really, I don't miss a lot. I mean, I love my parents and all, but I almost never feel like I want to be back there. I want to be here, playing music. Period.

CHEYENNE BELLE

I miss my sisters.

When I'm gone for a long time and then go back home, it's like everyone and everything has changed. I mean, I'll leave and Katherine will be into dolls and cartoons, and I'll come back and she's into pop music and makeup. (Bad pop music and too much makeup. I need to get Theresa the hell away from her.) It's kind of mind-blowing.

RICHIE MCGILL

My dad. He's all alone since my mom died. I wish I was there for him more. But he's proud of me, and that means everything.

HARBINGER JONES

For the first time ever, the Scar Boys had a gig on New Year's Eve.

It turns out that New Year's Eve gigs are hard to come by. They pay like three times what a normal gig pays, and every band, every accordion player, every novelty act featuring pigeons and balloons and scarves, wants one.

Our gig was thanks to our new manager, Jeff. We'd been clients for maybe three weeks, and already it was paying dividends.

A club in Tribeca, a part of the city we'd never really explored, had a last-minute opening. The guitar player for one of four bands on the bill, Here's the Beef, had been arrested. The poor guy was going to be welcoming in 1987 from a jail cell. "Possession," Jeff said. "Let that be a lesson to you." Jeff loved to say stuff like that: "Let that be a lesson to you." "I hope you learned something here." "Give a man a fish and he eats dinner; teach a man to fish and he eats for a lifetime." Truth is, after a while that crap wore on my nerves. I think all four of us looked at Jeff as a kind of kung fu master. He was wise. We were idiots. Only half of that turned out to be true.

We were scheduled to go on at 1:00 a.m., which for a New York City New Year's Eve party is actually pretty good. The only better slot is to be the band onstage at midnight. But it also meant we had a lot of time to sit around and wait.

Johnny and Chey were camped out at the bar, talking quietly, while Richie and I watched the other bands. I decided to take a cigarette break at 11:55, making sure I was outside when midnight came. Johnny and Cheyenne had seemed to reach some kind of truce, and I didn't really want to watch them ring in the new year with a kiss.

CHEYENNE BELLE

Every time a person thinks she hits bottom, she finds a new flight of stairs leading down. The stairs that New Year's Eve were especially long.

It's funny, because the night actually started out pretty good. We got there early, unloaded our gear, and checked out the club. It was called the One More Chance Saloon—the name was a joke on something called the Last Chance Saloon. Or at least that's what Harry said.

Anyway, it was a smallish, square-shaped room with a tiny stage up front. There was a bar on the left-hand side and a balcony on three sides looking down on a dance floor. There were already a bunch of people there, and the vibe, like it always is before midnight on New Year's Eve, was good.

The first band on the bill was just getting started.

"Hey." Johnny was standing next to me but had his eyes on the stage when he spoke.

"Hey," I answered. He and I hadn't talked since my

freak-out in Harry's backyard, and I felt pretty bad about it. "Look, Johnny," I began. I wanted to apologize and wanted to thank him for the guitar pick, but he held up his palm and turned to face me.

"Hi," he said, extending his other hand. "I'm Johnny McKenna." He smiled. It was the old Johnny smile. The smile I fell in love with. "Can I buy you a drink?"

And just like that, a month of feeling bad about us was wiped away. Well, not wiped away, but watered down.

"I would love a drink," I said, shaking his hand. I led him to the bar.

The club was pretty lax about carding. Whether that was because we were in one of the bands or because it was New Year's Eve, I don't know. Either way, they barely glanced at our fake IDs and served us each a beer.

Johnny and I made small talk. We talked about the club and how we both felt at home in places like that. We talked about Richie's new motorcycle and what we thought that might mean for his skateboard. We talked about Jeff.

"Has Harry seemed distant lately?" Johnny asked when there was a lull in the conversation.

"What do you mean?"

"I don't know. It's like his heart hasn't really been in the band lately."

I couldn't tell if Johnny was upset, worried, or just curious about Harry, but I didn't really care. Talk of Harry was going to ruin the mood, so I steered the conversation in a different direction.

"Thanks for the pick." I was wearing the pick he'd given me for Christmas on a silver chain around my neck, and I showed him. Johnny leaned over and gave me a slow and gentle kiss on the cheek, letting his lips linger for just an extra second. He pulled back and smiled. It was a beautiful smile.

I don't know how long we were sitting there, but I saw that my glass was empty, while Johnny's was mostly full. I flagged the bartender, and she poured me another.

We kept talking, the beer and Johnny both giving me a warm feeling inside. We talked about how well he had done with his physical therapy. We talked about my new job at the bookstore and how much I liked it.

"You know, you never told me why you decided to get a job," he said.

I couldn't tell him the real reason, so I just said, "I was bored." I guess the answer was good enough, because he nodded.

Johnny was about a third done with his beer when my glass was empty again. Now I was feeling great. I waved my hand, and another pint appeared in front of me. The buzz in the room was starting to build as the clock crept toward midnight.

We talked some more, except now I think I was doing

most of the talking. I honestly don't remember what I said, but when I looked up again, Johnny still had some beer in his glass and I was on my fourth. Or was it my fifth?

"Chey?" Johnny asked. And now the room was starting to spin a bit. "I think maybe you've had enough."

That was classic Johnny. Not *don't you think maybe you've had enough?* No. I *think you've had enough.*

I just waved my hand like I was literally brushing him off. "Lighten up, Johnny. I'm fine."

He let it drop until the bartender was putting yet another beer in front of me. This time, Johnny talked to her.

"Don't you think she's had enough?" The bartender, a skinny white girl barely able to keep up with all the people ordering drinks, stopped and looked at me.

"You okay, sugar?" she asked.

"I'm fine," I said, though I wasn't sure that either of those words came out as something another human being could understand. I think they might've sounded more like whale song.

The bartender shrugged her shoulders and turned to the next customer. I wasn't her sister or her daughter or her girlfriend, so I wasn't her problem.

I stuck my tongue out at Johnny, trying, I thought, to be playful.

He looked at me, shook his head, and mumbled, "Happy New Year, Cheyenne Belle." Then he walked away.

HARBINGER JONES

I was leaning against the outside wall of the club, smoking, when I heard the New Year's countdown begin. I'm big on symbolism, and I felt like the whole world was counting down to the beginning of my new life. It reminded me of the day of the thunderstorm. That day, I was counting Mississippis after each flash of lightning, trying to figure out how far away the storm was. A part of me thought that this new countdown would finally wipe that one away. Stupid, I know, but I thought it just the same.

"Ten!" came the muffled shout, from not only inside the club but from half the apartments in earshot.

"Nine!" I closed my eyes and tried to picture where I would be in twelve months.

"Eight!" Would I be standing outside some bar, waiting for another gig?

"Seven!" Would I be home from college for the Christmas break and watching the ball drop on TV with my parents?

"Six!" The door to the club slammed open, and a drunk girl came stumbling out, landing both hands on a car parked right in front of me.

"Five!" She hurled. Right on the car.

"Four!" I tried to go back to actualizing my future, but the damage was done and I was pulled out of the moment.

"Three!"

"Oh, shit!" the girl said. She looked around in a panic, like something was wrong. "You!"

"Two!" She took a step forward and grabbed me by the collar.

"Prepare to be kissed," she slurred in my face.

"One!" And the girl planted a big, sloppy, vomit-ridden kiss on me. What is it about girls and me and throw-up? She took a step back and looked at me for the first time. "Whoa," she said. "I must be more drunk than I thought."

There were two obvious choices: One, I could just push the girl away and go back inside, thoroughly disgusted. Or, two, I could make out with her.

I did the only thing I was wired to do. Option three, try to be the nice guy.

"Are you okay?" I asked. "Can I help you?"

She mumbled the words *New Year's* and staggered back to the party raging inside the club.

RICHIE MCGILL

When the clock struck midnight, I was hanging with this crowd of fans and we all clanked glasses, high-fived, and hugged. It was pretty cool. Then, out of nowhere, this drunk chick stumbled in from outside and planted a big nasty kiss on me. I say nasty because she tasted like puke. It was pretty gross.

"Happy New Year's," she muttered, and stumbled away. I found out only later that it was probably the same girl who'd kissed Harry outside. I like to freak him out by telling him that when she kissed me right after kissing him, it was like me and him kissing. The dude is such a prude. Cracks me up every time.

HARBINGER JONES

When I went back inside a few minutes after midnight—my impromptu date thankfully nowhere to be seen—I found Johnny sitting alone at a table near the front, nursing a beer. Richie was at the bar with a bunch of people, and Chey wasn't anywhere in my line of sight.

"Happy New Year," I said. Johnny just nodded in response.

"You okay?" I asked.

"I don't know," Johnny answered, looking at his shoes. "I'm just so tired, Harry."

I figured he meant tired of the ups and downs with Cheyenne, or maybe that the long night was too much strain on his leg. Whatever it was, he just seemed so sad.

After a minute, Johnny let out a big sigh and pushed himself up from the table. "Let's go tune your guitar to the keyboard."

And we did.

CHEYENNE BELLE

I don't want to talk about the actual gig.

I don't remember a lot. And what I do remember, I don't want to talk about. The other guys can give you what you need on that one.

HARBINGER JONES

It was the worst gig we ever played, or ever would play, mostly because Chey was falling-down drunk. And by falling-down drunk, I mean that she couldn't stand up.

When the band before us started breaking down equipment, we gathered by the side of the stage, ready to move our gear up quickly. Johnny was motionless, lost in his own thoughts. Richie was a ball of nervous energy, rat-a-tat-tatting his sticks against his thigh. I had my guitar slung over my back and my hat pulled low, trying, but failing, to look cool.

I figured Chey was in the bathroom and didn't pay it much mind until we had all our equipment—including her bass and her amp—on the stage.

"Where is she?" I asked. Johnny was just about to answer, a look of resignation on his face, when Chey stumbled up the stairs on the side of the stage. I reached out and caught her before she nose-dived into Richie's mounted toms.

When she looked up at me, her eyes were sparkling, but not the kind of sparkling that made me fall for her. Maybe *glassy* would be a better word. Her eyes were glassy. Or maybe *swimming* would be the best word. Her eyes were swimming.

"Are you high?" I asked.

"No," Johnny offered from his seat on the cramped stage behind me. "She's drunk."

"Oh, shit," I mumbled. "Can you play?" I talked to her like she was an imbecile, and that made Chey laugh.

"A courz Icahn play," she slurred. She gained her footing, found her bass, and put it on. The weight of the instrument against her small frame was too much, and Chey fell backward onto her amp. She caught herself so she landed on her butt, and it looked more like she sat down roughly than anything else. She giggled.

"Johnny," I asked, turning to him, "what do we do?"

He looked at me, looked at Cheyenne, and shook his head. "We play."

Richie shrugged and played the opening drum fill to the first song on our set list: tonight, a cover of the Beatles' "Birthday" with *New Year* substituted for *birthday* each time the word came up in the song. It was a short drum fill and ended with all of the instruments crashing in together. And that's just what Cheyenne did. She crashed in.

She was late with the riff and was playing the wrong key. I tried to shout to her, but her eyes were closed and she was lost in the music, hearing, I guess, what her beer-soaked brain wanted her to hear.

Each song after that was worse than the one that came before.

At the end of the fifth song, Johnny said, "Thanks, and Happy New Year, everyone," and walked off the stage.

"Pussy!" Cheyenne yelled after him, and she launched into "Girl in the Band."

I had no idea what to do, and I don't think Richie did, either. There were really only two choices. Follow Johnny off the stage, or stay and play.

We stayed and played with me singing lead. We got through two more songs, sort of, before it became clear that Cheyenne was done.

There was a smattering of polite applause, with a couple of "You guys suck" chants thrown in for good measure. Luckily, people didn't need the Scar Boys to feel good that night. Or at least they did a pretty good job of pretending to feel good. I have a theory that everyone secretly hates New Year's Eve as much as I do, but that no one will admit it. Mandated pleasure is an oxymoron.

We left the stage, and that was that. I was pretty sure it was the end of the Scar Boys.

RICHIE MCGILL

New Year's Eve was brutal. I mean, fucking brutal.

Cheyenne was, like, ten sheets to the wind, Johnny was being a whiny bitch, and Harry was just Harry. Definitely the worst gig we ever had. I mean, Johnny walked offstage halfway through.

But you know what? I still would've rather been playing that God-awful gig than doing just about anything else. That's how much I love this band.

HARBINGER JONES

It was two weeks before we all saw each other again.

I spent most of that time lying low and trying to put the finishing touches on my essay. The focus of the piece was the Scar Boys and what a life-changing experience that had been, but I didn't want to end it on the down note of the New Year's Eve gig. I was up to the part where Johnny lost his leg and didn't know where to go next.

When the phone rang, I was lying on my bed reading and rereading what I'd written, figuring this must be what people call writer's block. It was Jeff; he was summoning the entire band to a diner on the west side of New York City the following day. He was brief, he was matter-of-fact, and he hung up.

All thoughts of the essay went temporarily out of my head.

RICHIE MCGILL

I figured the band was toast, so I was surprised when Jeff called me. "Come to such-and-such diner tomorrow," he said.

"Why?" I asked.

"Why not?" he answered. "What have you got to lose?"

Dude had a point, so I went.

HARBINGER JONES

Richie, Johnny, and I drove downtown in silence, only the sound of the Replacements' *Let It Be* keeping us company. I'd chosen that record on purpose. The title of the album came from the Beatles record of the same name, the latter an unintended chronicle of the demise of the greatest rock band of all time. Since I was pretty sure I was going to a funeral—not a wake; there's too much laughing at wakes, and this was not a day for laughing—it seemed fitting. The choice of music was a pretty subtle inside joke that I think was lost on the other guys.

Honestly, I didn't think Cheyenne would show up, but there she was, sitting in the booth with Jeff when we arrived. She looked awful. She was bundled in a winter coat, her hair was a rat's nest, and the sunglasses on her face couldn't hide the bags under her eyes or the sallow look of her cheeks. Johnny and I both slid in the booth next to Jeff, wanting, each for our own reasons, to put distance between us and Cheyenne, as if that hadn't happened already.

Jeff stayed mostly quiet until after we ordered and our food had arrived. He was polite, making small talk, chitchat. Then, just as I was sinking my teeth into a French fry smothered in brown gravy, a Maryland delicacy that had followed me home from the road, he let loose.

"What the fuck were you little knuckleheads thinking?" Jeff had never talked to us like this before. He was always in sales mode, in teaching mode, in wise-mature-adult mode. Not today.

"Don't look at us," Johnny said. "Look at her." He nodded his chin in Cheyenne's direction. She didn't respond in any way. She simply had a sip of her coffee and kept her head down.

"Oh, I know," he continued. "Chey got drunk. Which was really stupid," he added, turning to her. "She and I have discussed this at length, and I'm confident it won't happen again. Right, Cheyenne?"

"Right," she answered. Her voice was thin, weak.

"But maybe Cheyenne wouldn't be getting drunk at gigs if you boys didn't shit where you eat."

"Huh?" Richie was sincerely confused.

"It means don't diddle your fellow bandmates."

"Hey, man, I'm not really sure what you mean by *diddle*, but I ain't never—"

"Put a sock in it, drummer boy. You all know what I'm talking about. I have no idea who has relationships with who in this band, and I don't want to know. What I do know is that all this behind-the-scenes shit is fucking everything up. So, from today forward, you're no longer friends; you're business partners. Understand?"

It took me a minute to process that.

"I'm sorry, Jeff, did you say you don't want us to be friends?" I asked.

"That's right."

No one else jumped in, so I continued, "But aren't our friendships what make the chemistry of the band work?"

He smiled. Like a shark. "No. They're not. What makes the band work is the chemistry of the music."

"I don't know—" I started, but he cut me off.

"Cheyenne," Jeff said, turning to her, "how close are you and Mr. Drummer Boy, over here?"

"Dude," Richie said, "stop calling me that."

Cheyenne thought about it for a minute. "I don't know. Not that close, I guess."

Jeff turned to Richie.

"What?" Richie asked, his hackles now up.

"Well, is she right?"

"I don't know. We see each other all the time. She's, like, one of my best friends."

"Do the two of you ever hang out outside the band? Do you go to movies together or anything?"

"No," Richie answered.

"Do you call each other on the phone to talk?"

"No."

"Do you even have Cheyenne's phone number?"

"No." Richie hung his head.

"Buck up, Drummer Boy. This is a good thing. Let me ask one last question. How close are you and Cheyenne musically?"

Richie scrunched his face as he thought about this. "I'd say we're married." He flashed a grin at Cheyenne, and she grinned back. Johnny was sitting next to me, and I could feel the air around us shrivel.

"That's right. You and she are musical soul mates. It's a beautiful thing. But once the amps are off, you hardly know each other. That, kiddies, is what you will now strive for. It's what you need to become. You are fellow musicians, and you are business partners. Once you learn how to do that, maybe, just maybe, you can go back to being friends. Everyone understand?"

And we did.

CHEYENNE BELLE

A couple of days before Jeff had dragged the whole band to New York City for lunch, he'd taken me out to a kind of fancy restaurant where Central Avenue crosses the border into Scarsdale. Well, fancier then I was used to anyway. It was a Red Lobster. Have you heard of these places? I actually got to eat lobster! That was a first for me. I thought it was gross but didn't want to say anything. I wanted to be sophisticated.

"Look," Jeff said after we'd ordered. "I don't care if you drink. In fact, here." He slid a glass of white wine from in front of his place setting to in front of mine. I looked at the glass and at Jeff like they weren't real. "I only care that whatever you do offstage doesn't hurt what's happening onstage. Do you understand?"

I nodded. Jeff was twenty-eight-years old, and I took him very seriously.

"Good," he said. "Moderation and control are important lessons to learn, Cheyenne."

"Can I ask you something?" I was afraid to sip the wine—afraid that it might not be real, that it might be a trap—and wanted to distract myself.

"Sure, kid, shoot."

"Why does any of this matter? Isn't the band kind of, I don't know, over?"

"What? No, no. Great bands go through this shit all the time." I liked the way Jeff cursed, like swear words were just words. "Roger Waters and David Gilmour can't be in the same room with each other."

"But didn't Pink Floyd break up?"

"Yeah, but they were together for years hating each other, and they made zillions."

"Okay, but what about Johnny and Harry? I'm pretty sure they think this is over. I haven't even talked to them since New Year's Eve."

"Leave them to me, okay?"

I trusted Jeff. I don't know why, but I did. "Okay," I answered.

It was a little weird he was sitting on the same side of the booth as me, but I just figured that was how older people went to dinner in fancier restaurants. Anyway, that's when he suggested I get a tattoo.

"You want me to get a what?" I said.

"A tattoo."

"Why?"

"This is the Scar Boys, Cheyenne. A tattoo *is* a scar."

I liked that. I know this sounds completely crazy, but I was kind of envious of Johnny's and Harry's scars. If you'd've asked Johnny if he could've had his leg back, of course he would've said yes. Harry would have wanted to be rid of his scars, too. But what had happened to them made them closer, tied them to the music, tied them to each other. It gave them an identity. There was something cool about it.

But I still had my doubts.

"The only kids who have tattoos are super hardcore punks or *Rocky Horror* fans," I told Jeff. "That's not us at all."

"I know. That's what makes it so cool. You guys have this totally badass, dysfunctional image, and then the most amazing and accessible rock and roll comes out of your instruments. We need to play up the former to emphasize the latter."

I thought about it for a minute. "Does it hurt?"

He rolled up his sleeve and showed me his own tattoo. It was a green-and-black line drawing of a pyramid with an eye on top. "Hell, yes, it hurts," he said. "But it's like a badge of honor. You become a member of a secret club."

I liked the sound of that, too. "Does that mean anything?" I asked, pointing at his pyramid. He opened his wallet, took out a dollar bill, and showed me the back.

"It's where mysticism and money come together," he said. Jeff was always talking about money.

Anyway, a week later, when the band finally rehearsed again, I was sporting a new tattoo at the base of my spine. I wore a shirt that was a bit small on me, knowing that every time I turned around, the guys would get a glimpse of the new art. I hardly said two words through the whole rehearsal, but I must've turned around, like, fifteen times. Every time I did, I tried to sneak a peek at my bandmates.

Harry was in his own world with the guitar, and Johnny

just sat staring into space, looking down every so often to write in this little black book he'd started carrying around. Richie saw the tattoo, though. He shook his head and smiled at me when the other guys weren't looking.

I know Harry and Johnny saw it, too, but neither one ever said anything. I guess this was the new world Jeff wanted—business partners, not friends. But . . .

Well, Jeff's whole "no-friends" rule. He was kind of full of shit.

That night at Red Lobster, he kept pouring me glasses of wine, and I kept drinking them.

And he and I made out in his car.

And then we went back to his apartment in New York City.

HARBINGER JONES

We were all business at that rehearsal. No one looked anyone else in the eye, except for Richie. We were all looking not just at him, we were looking to him. It was like the gravitational center of the band, which had once revolved around the planetary system of me and Johnny, with Johnny Jupiter and me one of his moons, had shifted to a spot that hovered just below and to the left of Richie's crash cymbal.

I think Richie was kind of freaked out by it, but he didn't say anything. We were taking Jeff's words to heart and were there to play music, nothing more. It was awkward, it was stilted, it was even painful at points. But here's the thing. I kind of loved it.

When you stripped all that other shit away—the broken, repaired, and rebroken friendship between me and Johnny; the broken, repaired, and rebroken relationship between Chey and Johnny; my unrequited love for Cheyenne—when all that nonsense was gone, locked in a drawer with no key, when only the music was left, it was a beautiful thing.

But that was only true while we were actually playing music. The moments in between the songs at that rehearsal were torture. I reverted all the way back to my thirteen-year-old self and hardly said two words. Johnny, his face a blank slate, devoid of any emotion, barely spoke. Cheyenne didn't engage with any of us in any way between the songs, though she kept turning around, making sure we all saw her new tattoo. If she wasn't going to say anything about it, neither was I, but, really, I thought it was pretty cool.

It was a severed leg with a lightning bolt on it. That girl has bravado. You have to love that. The rest of the time, she sat on her amp and plucked the bass, only looking up when the next song started.

The moments without music were like those first moments all these years ago between decreasing doses of methadone as Dr. Kenny weaned me off. But when the music started, man, oh, man, it worked. It just worked.

RICHIE MCGILL

That was the weirdest rehearsal ever.

I mean, Scar Boys rehearsals always went the same way: we would sit and wait for Johnny to tell us what to do. Maybe every so often, one of us would get a bug up our ass to play a certain song and just launch into it, but most of the time Johnny led the way. And if Johnny wasn't all there, like right after the thing with his leg, Harry would step in.

At that rehearsal, the first one after Jeff bawled us out, the other guys just sat there, looking at me. I'm thinking, like, *What the fuck did I do?* And they're still just looking at me. Then I figured it out. They were all so caught up in their own stupid shit that they were waiting for me to take over. I'm the drummer, for chrissakes. I mean, yeah, Don Henley and Phil Collins do that shit, but I'm more of a Keith Moon–Tommy Ramone kind of dude. Leading wasn't my thing.

Harry was twitchy, looking like he wanted to say something but couldn't or wouldn't; Chey kept her head down, turning around every so often so we could see her new tattoo; and Johnny kept writing in this little black book. It was the kind of book that Fonzie used to keep girls' phone numbers in. It was the first time I ever noticed it, but I don't think I ever saw him without it after that. Every time there was a break in the music, Johnny opened the book and started scribbling stuff down. It was like he was getting lost in the words or something. When I looked more closely, I could see that the book wasn't new. He had it opened to the middle, and it was kind of bent and worn. He caught me looking and covered it up like it was some big secret.

I didn't think anything of it at the time.

Cheyenne's tattoo, by the way, was maybe the coolest thing I'd ever seen. It was so badass. I went out two days later and got my own. It's in a place that only a special few have gotten to see.

HARBINGER JONES

No matter what Jeff said, no matter what kind of nonsense was going on between the four of us—well, really, the three of us, because Richie was immune to all of it—these people were my friends. They were practically my family.

You know how I could tell? The music. Total strangers or business partners, or whatever it was we were supposed to be, can't make music like that. They just can't.

What we had was special.

I'd been struggling to find an ending to my fifty-thousand-word college essay, and it was then, while playing music at the first rehearsal after the New Year's debacle, that I figured it out.

I couldn't go to college. Of course I couldn't go to college. I wasn't craving some sort of conventional experience that prepared for me an even more conventional existence. The world told me a long time ago that it would not let me conform to its established norms, so why should I start now?

Maybe I was a coward. And maybe my face was a mangled piece of meat that scared children and small animals. And maybe I had a rougher go of it than seemed fair, but I had something else, too. Even with all the shit that was swirling around the Scar Boys, I had friends and I had purpose.

Johnny, Chey, and I had worked through stuff before, and we would work through stuff again. It might take time, but we would get back to a better place. I could feel it in my bones. I would just bide my time while it all sorted itself out.

Until then I would find joy and peace in the music, just like Johnny and I did that first day we played together after Georgia. That moment—the two of us in his bedroom, me playing guitar and him singing, with no structure, no rules, no bullshit, all the baggage left at the door—is one of the happiest moments of my life. If the University of Scranton, or anyone else, wanted to really understand me, they needed to understand that. I had my ending.

I finished the essay that night and mailed the package the following day. Even though I'd decided not to go to college, I submitted the application to Scranton anyway. I figured I owed my parents that much. And, hey, it never hurts to keep your options open.

PART EIGHT.
JANUARY TO MARCH 1987

It was a job, and I was just doing my job.
—Johnny Ramone

What's the dumbest thing you've ever done?

CHEYENNE BELLE
Duh, getting knocked up.

HARBINGER JONES
Letting a bunch of older kids tie me to a tree during a thunderstorm. I mean, I didn't even put up a fight. I'm not sure it would have turned out different if I had fought back. Who knows, maybe I would've been beaten up and then tied to a tree and almost struck by lightning anyway, but at least I would've tried to do something about it.

RICHIE MCGILL
This interview.

Nah, I'm just kidding. The dumbest thing I ever did was not tell my mom I loved her when I had the chance. She died of cancer when I was a little kid. By the time the end came, she looked so skinny and so sick that I was afraid of her. Think about how fucked up that is, a little kid being scared of his own mom.

When she was about to go into surgery, my dad tried to get me to go wish her luck and tell her how much I loved her, but I wouldn't do it. I just stayed in the hospital waiting room, reading comic books. My dad didn't push it. He let me hang out there with my aunt.

My mom died during the operation.

For a long time, I thought it was my fault, that if I'd told her I loved her, maybe she would've lived.

I told my dad all that a few years later, and it was the only time, other than my mom's funeral, that I saw him cry.

CHEYENNE BELLE

Things settled down for the next two months. We were back to a pretty routine schedule of rehearsing, and when I wasn't rehearsing, I was at the bookstore. I'd kept the drinking mostly under control, only occasionally letting it get bad, and was feeling pretty good about things.

Jeff kept pressuring me to crash at his apartment. I said yes sometimes, but a lot of times I said no. I felt mature and grown-up with Jeff, but I also felt pretty bad.

The only boy I'd ever slept with before Jeff was Johnny, and that ended with me having a miscarriage and him losing his leg. I mean, he didn't lose his leg because we had sex, but in my mind, everything was all twisted together in one of those crazy tight knots that you can never seem to unravel, you know?

The first time Jeff and I were together—and, really, most of the times we had sex—I was so drunk that I barely remembered it. I had this feeling in the pit of my stomach that was more than nerves and less than nausea. There was no real pleasure in it for me, other than knowing that I could still please someone else. And for whatever reason, that mattered to me. I felt broken, and being able to please someone else made me, on some level, feel whole again. I guess that's kind of messed up.

I was also terrified that Harry and Johnny would find out. They would've both freaked out.

But then again, maybe not.

The Scar Boys was a completely different band than it used to be. We were still tight musically—in some ways, tighter than ever—but the joy had gone out of playing. It was turning into a job.

I told that to Jeff on one of the few nights I did stay in the city.

"That's good," he said. "It should feel like a job. You guys need to understand what a slog this is going to be." *Slog.* Another Jeff word.

He was standing in the kitchen of his apartment—he called it a railroad flat, whatever that was—wearing only tighty whities and a smile. I had kind of hoped that grown men wore something better under their clothes, but maybe that was only in movies.

The apartment was long and narrow, with hardwood floors and exposed-brick walls. There were framed concert posters everywhere, giving the space just the right amount of cool. It's exactly what a girl like me thought a New York City apartment was supposed to look like. Except for the roaches. Lots of roaches. More roaches than should be allowed to live in one place. Jeff spread this white powder called Borax along the floorboards to kill them, but I'm not sure it worked. It might've helped if he'd ever bothered to clean a dish in his sink.

"But if this isn't fun, why does anyone do it?" I asked.

"Have you ever worked a real job?"

"You know I work at the bookstore."

"Yeah, well, I'm not sure that sitting around all day and reading books and talking about James Joyce Oates or whoever is work."

"That's not how it is at all in a boo—"

"Trust me. I know what I'm talking about."

There was a bit of Johnny in Jeff. When a conversation was closed, it was closed. Because he was older, I went along with it. Plus, he let me drink when we were at his place.

"When are you going to get us another gig?" I asked.

"Funny you should bring that up."

I waited.

"I just found out today and was waiting for the right time to tell you."

"Yeah?"

"I got you a gig opening for another band."

He was having fun stringing this out, and I let him.

"A pretty cool band."

I waited.

"At a pretty cool club."

The long pause this time was more than I could take. "Well?"

"Thursday, Friday, and Saturday nights, May seventh, eighth, and ninth, the Scar Boys will be opening for . . ."

"Oh, c'mon!"

"Drum roll, please."

"Jeff!"

"The Fleshtones. Three nights at Irving Plaza."

"What?" I was blown away. "Really?"

"Really. And it wasn't an easy gig to get. Usually, the label wants that spot for another band on their roster, but I talked them down in price."

"How much?"

"You guys are doing it for free."

I didn't care, and I'm pretty sure the other guys weren't going to care, either. I ran over to Jeff and gave him a monster hug. "We have to tell the other guys right now!"

"No, we can let that wait 'til tomorrow." He looked me in the eyes, took me by the hand, and started to lead me to the end of the apartment with the bed.

"Wait," I said. He stopped and looked at me again. "I need more wine."

HARBINGER JONES

Not surprisingly, the faceless admissions professional at the University of Scranton didn't appreciate my fifty-thousand-word application essay, and a form rejection letter was dispatched. Quickly, I might add.

I showed it to my parents. They didn't know that I had sent the school a book-length treatise on my life and assumed that the rejection had to do with my grades, my SAT scores, and my having taken a year off. My dad kept harping on that last one.

"It was a waste of a year, Harry," he blustered in my general direction one afternoon. "I'm sorry you didn't get into Scranton, but I'm not surprised." He held my gaze and sized me up. "You need a Plan B."

Plan B was the same as Plan A: play music. It's what I was meant to do. Can you imagine Jimmy Page if he hadn't played guitar? Can you picture him with short hair, in a suit and tie, doing data entry at some accounting firm?

My dad's idea of Plan B was for me to take classes at the local community college, the same place the rest of the high school misfits and miscreants wound up. It was like a holding pen for people who grew up to amount to something less than they were supposed to be.

Community college: dreams not welcome.

Sure, some kids made the most of it, putting their time in and transferring to a four-year college, and good for them. But I didn't have any illusions. For me, it would be like a Roach Motel. If I checked in, I would never check out.

Even knowing that, I agreed to my father's version of Plan B and registered for a writing course that summer. The whole exercise of the Scranton application essay showed me how much I liked to write, and I figured why not.

So other than trying to keep my parents (mostly my dad) off my back about school and about getting a job, I spent my mornings sleeping, my afternoons rehearsing, and my nights playing computer games. It developed into a kind of seamless routine that bordered on becoming a rut. If it wasn't for Richie's school schedule and my dad being gone four nights a week, I'm not sure I would've been able to tell you what day it was.

The rehearsals were great musically but otherwise lifeless. I know that sounds like a contradiction, because, really, music is life, but that's the way it was.

Cheyenne added three more tattoos, but still not one word about them was mentioned. It's like they had become logos for our newfound lack of friendship. Any acknowledgment of Chey's body art would have been an overt act of intimacy, and that was simply not allowed.

Except for when we returned from Georgia, those two months were the longest period of time we'd gone, since early in the eleventh grade, without a gig and without working on a new song. Newness had no place in what we were doing. We had gone from being an organism to being a machine.

The rehearsals became so repetitive that my brain would sort of check out. I found myself going back to old habits and running through lists in my head while I mindlessly strummed the chords to our songs. It's amazing how quickly the details of a list can leave a person's brain. I used to know every world capital cold. Now I was struggling with some of the easy ones. Was Lusaka the capital of Zambia or Zimbabwe?

Chey and Richie were the only two members of the band to really engage one another, and that was only while we were playing and it was only with their eyes and smiles. They really are the greatest rhythm section I've ever seen.

Johnny worried me. He looked thinner and twitchier as each week went by. His personal hygiene was going to shit—his hair was uncombed, his shirts were stained, and I could smell his breath from all the way across the room—and he was starting to walk with a limp, like he hadn't been doing his exercises. It reminded me of what he was like right after he lost his leg, when he was going through the trauma of figuring out how to live as an amputee. And it reminded me of me, for so many years after the thunderstorm.

The only way we saw Johnny engage with the world

was through his keyboard, and by writing in that little book he'd started carrying around. He would open it between songs and scribble something down. None of us knew what. I tried to sneak a peak over his shoulder once, and he pulled it away, making sure I couldn't see.

Other than that, I never asked Johnny how he was doing, and he never offered. The rules were the rules. The truth is that I used Jeff's rules as an excuse, as a place to hide, a place where I didn't have any responsibility for my relationships or my friends. I think we all did.

The Scar Boys played on like that with no end in sight, like zombies, until Jeff summoned us back to the diner in New York City with "news."

I thought maybe it was a record deal. I violated the "not-friends" protocol and asked Richie and Johnny what they thought on the ride to the city.

"Don't know, dude. Record deal would be pretty cool, though," Richie answered.

"Johnny?"

"No clue. I just hope he isn't going to yell at us again."

And that was the whole conversation.

When we got to the diner, Jeff and Chey were already there.

Cheyenne had stopped riding in cars with me or Johnny. She would let Richie pick her up for rehearsal, but only if I was picking up Johnny. Since Johnny, Richie, and I were riding down together, she told Richie she'd meet us there.

Jeff and Chey were seated on the same side of the booth, which was weird, so Johnny, Richie, and I slid in across from them. Jeff had a shit-eating grin on his face, and though she was trying to hide it, Chey did, too.

"Welcome, kiddies, one and all," he said, holding his arms open wide like he was Tommy, from the movie, like we were his disciples.

"So what's going on?" I asked.

"Do you want to tell them?" Jeff turned to look at Cheyenne. The way he looked at her, the way she looked back—no, wait, strike that. Not the way she looked back— the way she let him look at her, I could tell there was something between them. I shot glances around the table and saw that Johnny and Richie could tell, too.

Johnny, who hadn't been saying a whole lot lately, put his hand on his journal and gritted his teeth. "So Cheyenne knows this news, whatever it is, already?"

"I got here first, and Jeff couldn't wait to tell me," she said without missing a beat. Jeff smirked at that, as if he was thinking, *Good little girl*. It was like a billboard that said, *I own this one*, and it made the mood at the table a million times worse.

Richie, being Richie, said, "So what's the news? Is it okay to shit where we eat now?"

Johnny let out one loud cackle, a laugh of derision,

hatred, and disrespect. It echoed among our water glasses and died a slow death.

"Easy there, champ," Jeff said. "Let's not ruin what is a happy moment for our little quintet."

"Quartet," Johnny shot back. "There are only four of us in this band. Right, Chey?"

Cheyenne didn't answer. Whatever was happening with her and Jeff, she'd been found out, and she was embarrassed.

I took a deep breath, once again tired of all the crap. "So what's this big news?"

That's when Jeff told us about the three nights opening for the Fleshtones at Irving Plaza. It was big news. By far the biggest news we'd ever had. And no one reacted. Not me, not Johnny or Chey, not even Richie. I think it put Jeff back on his heels, because he tried to keep selling the news to us.

"I've got some label guys coming out to see the show. I won't say it's like an audition, but you guys nail it and we may have an in to cut a demo for one of the big fish."

He wanted us to think this was going to be our big break, and it was hard not to agree. The relentless hours of practice, the gig after gig after gig, the years of sweat, tears, and fears had been to prepare for these three dates in May. Part of me wanted to do a little dance of joy, but given the pall cast over the table—it was toxic, like Toxic

Avenger toxic—the only thing that felt right was a low-key response. The dysfunction of the Scar Boys was like a living, pulsating thing.

I looked at Cheyenne. She was staring at her food, stealing occasional peeks at the rest of us, mostly Johnny.

Johnny gave Chey a long look, his face a chalkboard with nothing on it, impossible to read. Except for his eyes. His eyes said it all. He opened his book, started to write something, then thought better of it and closed the cover. I wanted to reach out and tell him it was all okay, but it felt like the time for that had passed. "Can we go now?" he asked me. I looked at Richie, who nodded.

"Yeah, okay. Rehearsal tomorrow at my house at the usual time, Chey, okay?"

She gave the barest nod of her head. I thought she was going to cry.

Jeff, as if to prove some kind of point, put his arm around Chey while we were getting up. What a jerk.

On the ride home from the city, I finally cracked.

"Hey, John," I asked, "you okay?"

He didn't answer, just stared out the window at the passing road. I didn't try again.

CHEYENNE BELLE

I wanted to crawl under a rock at that lunch.

Jeff was being so obvious, it's like he was peeing on his

territory to mark it, and I was his territory. I felt peed on. He didn't do anything like kiss me or even hug me, but he made it clear we were together.

Richie made a comment about "not shitting where you eat," which was Jeff's big thing after the New Year's Eve gig, and Johnny laughed. It was the first time in weeks I'd heard Johnny laugh. But it wasn't a happy laugh. It sounded mean.

Anyway, I took the train home after that and just wanted to slink to my bed and fall asleep. I made a point of walking past my snoring dad and his unfinished snifter of brandy, thinking for the first time that drinking would only make me feel worse.

I was wrong. I had Theresa for that.

She was in our room when I got home, talking on the phone. I ignored her, flung myself on my bed, and smushed a pillow over my ears. Didn't help; I could still hear her side of the conversation.

"Yeah, a miscarriage."

What? I thought.

"I know, she likes to pretend she's high and mighty, but she's a slut just like the rest of us. . . . I don't know, one of the deformed losers in her band. . . . No, not the one with the fucked-up face, the three-legged stool."

I couldn't believe it. I lifted my head up and looked at her.

"Are you serious?"

She covered the receiver with her hand. "Do you mind?
I'm on the phone."

"You're on the phone talking about my incredibly
personal shit."

She looked at me blankly, just sitting there, chewing
her cud. "So?"

"So it's my business. How would you like it if I told
people about your stillbirth?"

"You mean you didn't?"

I didn't have any answer, because I'd told Johnny, Harry,
and Richie about it. Though I may have jazzed up the story
a bit. But that was different; I don't remember calling her a
slut or making fun of the cretin who knocked her up.

"Who are you talking to anyway?"

"I don't know, just some guy."

"Just some guy? You're telling my deepest secrets to
just some guy?"

She smiled and shrugged.

The phone receiver was on the nightstand between our
beds, so I reached over and hung it up.

"Hey, what the fuck?"

I dropped back down and put the pillow back over
my head.

"Why don't you go and get drunk again, Cheyenne?
Or better yet, why don't you just drop dead? No one will
care." I heard Theresa leave the room.

My drinking was obvious enough for Theresa to notice. That was bad. I mean, she drank a lot, too, so I guess she knew the signs. But still.

The other thing she said, though, was so much worse, because she was right. Who would care if I was dead? My parents? No. My sisters? Maybe one or two of the younger ones, but there were enough of us to go around. Jeff? No, I was smart enough to know that he was using me. I was a replaceable part. If I was gone, he would find some other band with some other girl and use her, too. Johnny and I were so far gone that I thought he'd be relieved. Harry, too. The only person I could imagine missing me was Richie, and even then, only when we played music. I should just leave. Or even better, I should just end it.

It was a new low point for me, and the only answer I had to low points was alcohol. I got up and went into the living room. My mother was sitting there, and so was my little sister Joan. They were on the love seat next to my father, who was still snoring gently. They were caught up in *Wheel of Fortune*, ignoring me as I walked in. *Fuck them*, I thought. I went right to my father's brandy, took it in hand, and drained it.

The warm sensation spreading from my throat to my chest made me feel better. I retreated to my room and flopped on the bed. My mother and sister either didn't notice or didn't care that I had just done this incredibly ballsy thing, because no one followed me. That made me feel even worse.

RICHIE MCGILL

The lunch with Jeff was just more drama, and, really, for a dude who was supposed to be our older, wiser manager, he was making things a whole lot worse.

Anyways, I felt pretty bad for Johnny after that lunch. When Harry and I dropped him off, I thought he was going to cry.

But maybe it was just deserts. I mean John'd slept with Chey when he knew Harry was in love with her. Everyone knew it, but John didn't care. Maybe it was just a case of what goes around comes around.

CHEYENNE BELLE

I stayed on my bed for a long time, thinking about everything. My dad's glass of brandy had been really full—like four fingers' worth—and I hadn't eaten since lunch, so downing it quickly made the room spin a little. I was used to that feeling, and it didn't bother me. In some ways, I liked it.

I don't know how or why, but I found myself holding the phone and dialing Johnny's number. When I realized what I was doing, I decided to just go with it. What the hell, right?

"Hello?" His mother. Ugh.

"Hi, Mrs. McKenna, this is Cheyenne. Is Johnny there?"

"Just a minute." Her voice was flat, like she'd given up on being a bitch to me. Maybe she finally realized that me, Harry, and Richie were here to stay.

I heard someone pick up a receiver, then I heard it hang up again. I figured that Johnny'd picked up in one room and his mom had hung up in another. But there was no background noise and I started to wonder if I was listening to a dead line.

"Hello?" I said, not sure if I'd get an answer, so it made my heart skip a beat when I heard Johnny's voice.

"Hey, Pick."

He sounded awful. I mean, like, really, really awful.

"Johnny? Are you okay?"

There was a long enough stretch of silence that I thought maybe he'd hung up on me.

"Yeah, I'm okay. Just a little bit out of it. I think it's my meds."

"What meds?" I didn't know anything about Johnny taking any meds. It wasn't anything he'd shared with me, and I wondered if he'd gone down the same road I had.

"It's nothing." His voice was slow and soft, flowing from his mouth like molasses. "What's up?"

Right, what's up. I called him. I didn't know what was up. I had no idea what was up. I let my brain shut down so my mouth could take over.

"Johnny, look, I'm sorry I've been such a bitch lately."
More silence.

"I just don't want you to be mad at me." Wait, wasn't I mad at him, too? I had no idea where this was heading.

"I'm not mad at you anymore, Chey. It's all water under the bridge. Everything is water under the bridge."

Everything is water under the bridge? I thought. *What does that mean?*

"I'm really tired." He seemed so out of it that he was barely making sense. My buzz was strong enough that I don't think I really picked up on just how awful he sounded.

"Is there anything I can do?"

"Do?"

"I don't know, to help you feel better."

Another crazy long pause.

"Johnny?"

"Can you turn back time?" He whispered the question.

"John?" He was starting to freak me out. A lot.

"Me, either."

And then I started to cry. I don't know what set me off, but I wished I was there, sitting next to Johnny, on the couch in his living room. I wanted to hold him. The distance the phone was putting between us may as well have been the distance to the moon. I was so frustrated, so angry, and so sad all at the same time.

"I'm really sorry." I was crying harder now. "I'm sorry."

I didn't even know what exactly I was apologizing for.

No answer. No noise.

"Johnny?" I choked back my tears as best as I could. "Are you still there?"

"I'm really tired, Chey. I need to go lie down."

He was freaking me out so much that if he hadn't said what he said next, I think I would've called a cab and gone straight to his house.

"Say hi to Jeff for me." And he hung up.

I dropped the phone, turned my face into the pillow, and screamed and cried. I don't know how long I was like that, but it must've been a while, because I heard my mom shout, "Stop that blubbering!" I wanted to yell, "Fuck you," back at her, but I didn't have it in me. This had to be the bottom. I had to have reached the end. Things really couldn't get any worse.

PART NINE,
JANUARY TO MARCH 1987

A lot of people want to die for a lot of reasons.

—Johnny Thunders

What motivates you?

HARBINGER JONES

I don't know. If I'm being honest, I guess I'm constantly needing to prove to the world that I'm normal, that I'm just like everyone else, even though I'm not. I still haven't figured out how to embrace that.

RICHIE MCGILL

Sex, and rock and roll. I don't do drugs.

CHEYENNE BELLE

Knowing that I have to live every day like it's my last.

CHEYENNE BELLE

It was the next day, and sunlight was pouring down through a window set high in the wall of Harry's basement, bathing Richie and his drum kit in this beautiful ray of light. He was tapping a drumstick around the edge of his mounted tom and using the drum key to tighten the skin.

Johnny had told Richie that he was going to walk to rehearsal, so the three of us were going through our normal warm-up routines while we waited for him.

Harry was hunched over his electronic tuner, trying to get the A string on his Strat just right. I was waiting for him to finish so I could use the tuner, too.

HARBINGER JONES

Tuning a guitar is an art. It works best to get one string perfect and then tune all the rest to it.

The trick, and a lot of people don't know this, is to tune up, not down. You want to start with the strings a little flat and tighten the machines—those are the chrome doodads on the top of the guitar—rather than loosen them. For some reason, the guitar seems to hold its tune better that way.

I had just gotten the A string as close as I was going to get it and was starting on the rest of the strings when my mom walked in.

CHEYENNE BELLE

She was wearing black stirrup pants and a long white blouse cinched with a belt, and she had on earrings and makeup, like she was about to leave the house. The first thing I noticed was that her color was all wrong. Her skin matched her shirt, like she was sick. And her lower lip was quivering.

Mrs. Jones is usually a pretty happy person. It's like she doesn't want to waste her time on bad stuff. I always admired that about her, especially after everything she'd been through with Harry.

But one look at her and I knew something bad had happened.

HARBINGER JONES

My mom looked like she'd seen a ghost. Wait, strike that. She looked like she *was* a ghost. My first thought was that something had happened to my dad.

CHEYENNE BELLE

"Kids," Harry's mom said. "I have some bad news."

And then she started crying. I don't think any of us knew what to do, not even Harry. I snuck a peek at Richie, who looked as nervous as I felt. He looked back at me and shrugged.

RICHIE MCGILL

I had no idea what was going on. But I knew it wasn't good.

HARBINGER JONES

"Mom?" I put my guitar down and went to her, and she wrapped me in a hug and wouldn't let go. And she was crying.

I'd seen my mom cry plenty over the years. As happy as she tried to be, my mom was no stranger to waterworks, but this, this was different. Something was seriously wrong, and it was completely freaking me out.

CHEYENNE BELLE

I realized something.

She came into the room and said, "Kids, I have some bad news." Not "Harry, I have some bad news."

Kids.

HARBINGER JONES

"Mom?" I asked again, totally unable to keep the fear out of my voice. She regained enough composure to pull away from me and start over.

"Mrs. McKenna called. . . . Oh, fuck, I don't know how to say this."

My mom never cursed.

CHEYENNE BELLE

Harry's mom never cursed.

"It's Johnny," she said, choking on his name. She took a deep breath, put her hands at her sides, palms down, like she was trying to steady herself, and started again. "I'm so sorry, kids. Johnny is gone."

At first, I didn't know what she meant. *Gone where? He's not coming to rehearsal?* Then my brain caught up.

"Gone?"

The word was a sucker punch to my gut. All of a sudden I couldn't breathe.

I tried to will the universe into having Johnny just be gone from this house, gone from Yonkers, gone from the Scar Boys, even gone from my life, but not gone from the world. Johnny couldn't be gone like that. He was one of the things that made the world real, like air. Johnny was air for me, oxygen. Even though we hadn't really talked in months, he'd still been there. Johnny was gone and I couldn't breathe. There was no air.

RICHIE MCGILL

"How?" I asked. I mean, shit. I knew the answer. We all knew the fucking answer. But the whole scene was kind of like a car wreck. I couldn't stop looking and couldn't help myself from asking how.

CHEYENNE BELLE

I'd already forgotten Richie was in the room. I'd forgotten anyone was in the room except for me and Harry's mom. I craned my head to look at Richie, and his eyes were wet. I looked back to Mrs. Jones, waiting for her to say what I already knew.

HARBINGER JONES

Everything came crashing to the fore like a tidal wave—

that lost look Johnny had in his eyes all the time, that little black book he'd started carrying around, the way he was letting himself go. All the clues were there for anyone who bothered to look.

My mom sighed. It was almost a moan. "I'm so, so sorry. Johnny took his own life." Her voice croaked, and she started crying again.

CHEYENNE BELLE

All I could think about was my phone call with Johnny the night before. I could have stopped this. Oh, my fucking God, I could have stopped it.

The room started spinning, and without realizing how or why, I was on the ground.

RICHIE MCGILL

Chey fell to the floor. It was like the weight of it made her sit down hard on her ass. She landed with a thud. Everything was happening in slow motion.

HARBINGER JONES

A million thoughts about Johnny tried to push their way through to the surface: My confusion at how he could do such a thing. My morbid curiosity about how he did it. Was it pills? A gun? A rope? My wondering if he'd left a note, because that's what people who commit suicide are supposed to do. My anger at him for leaving without talking to me first. My anger at myself for not trying harder to talk to him. My heart breaking for his older brother, Russell, who loved Johnny so much. My own thoughts about suicide and how many times over the years, when I was younger and things were really bad for me, I wondered what it would be like and if it would make everything better. My wondering if it made things better for Johnny and then my hating myself for thinking that.

My endless lists of useless facts tried to come crashing in, too. Presidents and Oscar winners and SAT vocabulary words getting jumbled together and trying to drown out the screaming noise of the universe. All of the signal being replaced by noise, nothing but noise.

CHEYENNE BELLE

I screamed.

A bomb had been shoved down my throat and had exploded all of my insides. It made me break into a thousand pieces, all of them sharp and jagged. I was Humpty Dumpty and I was made of glass.

I could see a kind of swirling vortex opening up in front of me. It was black and gray, with flashes of lightning. It was filled with pain and misery, and it was where I wanted to be. All I wanted to do right then was follow Johnny and our baby into oblivion.

Every inch of me hurt, inside and out. From the soles of my feet to the hair on my head, I was a pulsing knot of hurt. I'd never known such pain. This was the miscarriage times a million. Times infinity.

HARBINGER JONES

Cheyenne's scream ripped a hole in me. It ripped a hole in the world.

I turned away from my mom, went to Chey, and knelt down beside her.

"Chey," I said, but I don't think she heard me.

"Chey." A little louder, still nothing. I touched her gently on the shoulder.

CHEYENNE BELLE

I looked up, and Harry was standing next to me. I never saw him cross the room, but somehow his hand was on my shoulder. That black vortex of death was trying to suck me in and pull me away from all of this, and that was what I wanted. I wanted it so bad.

The alternative, to keep going, to face what had happened, to live knowing that Johnny's suicide was all my fault, was more terrifying than oblivion. I was more afraid of living than of dying. Way more afraid. If I could just fall into the black hole, everything would be okay.

But I couldn't. Harry's hand was holding me firm to

the earth. Firm to the floor of his basement.

When I looked at him, Harry's eyes were floating in a sea of saltwater, and they were filled with worry and dread. Whether that was for Johnny, me, or all three of us, I didn't know. But Harry's eyes were real, they were something for me to hold on to. I grabbed hold and wouldn't let go.

RICHIE MCGILL

Harry's mom was on the ground, too. I didn't see her go down, but there she was, on the floor, crying like the rest of us. After everything that had happened to Harry, Mrs. J. must've worried about him doing something like this. Johnny had to be a knife in her fucking heart.

The whole scene was starting to freak me out big-time. I needed to do something.

HARBINGER JONES

Richie got up from behind the drums, walked over, and put a hand on my back. When I looked up, his face was streaked with tears and his cheeks were flush. He mouthed, "Are you okay? Should I go?" I nodded and silently thanked the God I didn't believe in for a friend like Richie McGill.

CHEYENNE BELLE

I buried my face in Harry's chest and screamed and cried. He just kept saying he was sorry and that it was going to be okay, over and over and over again. It was a lie, and we both knew it. Nothing was going to be okay, ever again.

RICHIE MCGILL

I helped Harry's mom up off the floor, partly to help her out of the room so Harry and Chey could have some space, and partly to get the fuck out of there myself. I felt like I was gonna puke or explode or something if I stayed in that basement one more minute.

Mrs. J. walked me to the entryway by the front door and gave me a long hug. She sniffled a few times but was starting to pull her shit together.

"Do you want to stay? Do you want me to call your father?"

"No, I'll be okay." I started to leave but then turned around. "Wait, do you want me to stay with you for a bit?"

She paused for a minute and then kind of hung her head and nodded. I swear to God she looked like a little kid.

I took her arm and led Mrs. J. to the kitchen. She made us both tea, we talked about Johnny, and we waited for Harry and Chey to come upstairs. We waited a long time.

CHEYENNE BELLE

I don't know how long Harry and I were on the floor, but when I looked up, Richie and Mrs. Jones were gone. I stayed there and cried until I felt like there must've been blood pouring out of my eyes. That was the last thing I remembered, thinking that there was blood pouring out of my eyes.

HARBINGER JONES

I held Chey until she fell asleep.

I stroked her hair while I thought about Johnny. I kept remembering the first day he and I met, and how he'd saved me from a bully. He'd swooped in and saved me like he was Superman. But he did more than save me from a bully.

When I met Johnny, I was a nothing, a nobody. No, wait, strike that. I was something worse. I was a pariah. At least a nobody can fade into the background. I couldn't do that because people couldn't help but notice me. Once Johnny and I found each other, all that changed.

In every way imaginable, Johnny McKenna saved my life.

But I couldn't save him.

I didn't even try.

It turns out I'm a nothing after all.

I cried until I fell asleep, too.

Chey and I stayed there like that, on the floor, in each other's arms. We were together, but we were broken, and we were, each of us, utterly and completely alone.

PART TEN,
MARCH 1987

I don't think Jimi committed suicide in the conventional way. He just decided to exit when he wanted to.
—Eric Burdon, on Jimi Hendrix

What do you miss most about Johnny McKenna?

HARBINGER JONES

Back when we were in middle school, we used to go running together. When we couldn't go any farther, we would flop down on some neighbor's lawn and catch our breath. Then we would just talk and laugh. We laughed a lot.

That's what I miss, his friendship.

RICHIE MCGILL

I don't know, I miss a lot of things. Mostly I miss how the guy lit up a room, or at least the way he did before he lost his leg. You can take that however you want, but the dude was a force of nature. You kind of felt proud that he'd picked you as a friend.

CHEYENNE BELLE

Everything.

HARBINGER JONES

Funeral homes are weird places. They're little factories for honoring the dead. Johnny's service was held at a place near our old high school; it was a long, low white house that, on the outside, looked inviting. One of the ways death tricks you, I suppose.

The wake was a scene. I mean, Johnny was insanely popular all throughout school, kind of like Ferris Bueller. When we went on the road and then when he lost his leg, the legend of Johnny McKenna only grew.

When I first walked into the room and saw the open casket at the far end, my stomach turned. The rest of the room seemed to blur at the edges, the whole thing collapsing into a kind of wormhole that led straight to the coffin. It took me a minute to get my bearings.

Rows of chairs had been set up like people were coming to see Johnny play one last show. There were pictures of him scattered on end tables next to the few upholstered chairs and couches. His keyboard was set up in a corner, with a pair of his old running shoes underneath. That bothered me a little. Johnny played the keyboard only because he couldn't wear those running shoes anymore. The symbolism was all screwed up.

Richie, Chey, and I had come to the wake together. Richie looked sharp in a new suit, while I stood there swimming in an ill-fitting gray two-piece with a skinny tie and pointy black boots. It was the same suit I had worn under my gown at our high school graduation. I was the only kid not smart enough to figure out that it didn't matter what you wore under your gown. Most everyone had worn shorts, and supposedly one kid, John Emmett, had been naked. Chey looked beautiful at the wake, like she always does, in her skirt and blazer. Though she did remind me of Jo from *Facts of Life*.

Like Scarecrow and the Tin Man protecting Dorothy, Richie and I each hooked one of Chey's arms and took our place in the line of mourners, waiting until it was our turn to approach the casket.

You always hear people say how dead bodies at wakes look peaceful. Johnny didn't look peaceful. He looked dead. The color in his cheeks was only there because someone had applied makeup, and his eyes were taped shut. The suit he was wearing didn't fit any better than the suit I was wearing.

I just bowed my head and told Johnny how sorry I was and that I hoped he was somewhere where he could run. As much as he loved music, Johnny's soul was connected to running the same way my soul was connected to the guitar. I didn't know what else to say or think.

Cheyenne started to cry pretty hard when we saw Johnny, and Richie and I tried to pull her away, but she stopped us. She reached into a small purse she had slung over her shoulder and gently dropped something in the casket. It fell to the side of Johnny's body, so I didn't see what it was. I never asked.

I'd love to tell you that it was more dramatic than that. That one of us made a speech or broke down or did something grandiose. We didn't. We paid our respects like everyone else, and we moved on. The moment demanded more, but there was no more to be done.

After saying our final good-byes, we followed the other mourners, like a morbid sort of conga line, to see Johnny's parents. His mother was barely holding it together as she greeted and hugged the people in front of us, an older couple, maybe some aunt and uncle of Johnny's. The four of them—the couple and Johnny's parents—talked for a moment that felt like a year, and then it was our turn.

Mrs. McKenna looked at Chey, Richie, and me with ice in her eyes. I thought for sure she was going to take a swing at me.

She did just the opposite.

Johnny's mother, the woman who had so detested us, literally fell into our arms, all six of our arms, and started wailing. She was saying something but was so upset I couldn't make it out at first.

"Thankyoubingsugofrnds" is what I heard. I could only mumble, "I'm so sorry," as I held her. She sucked in a big breath, and then her words resolved themselves.

"Thank you for being such good friends," she was

SCAR GIRL

saying over and over again. Mr. McKenna gently put a hand on his wife's shoulder, and she pulled back.

I was too choked up to speak, and as soon as I tried, I lost it. So did Chey. And so did Richie. The raw emotion of it was too much to handle. I wanted to tell Mrs. McKenna, I wanted to scream at her that we weren't the friends she thought we were. That we, along with everyone else, had let her son down. But I didn't. I couldn't.

We left Johnny's parents and went to the back of the room. I tried hard to regain some, any, sense of equilibrium.

Everyone was there. My parents, Richie's dad. Most of Chey's sisters and her parents, so many of the kids from school—the good ones and the sadistic dickheads alike—had all turned out to say good-bye to Johnny McKenna.

The three of us stayed in the back, sticking close to one another, trying to fend off the endless stream of mourners who wanted to offer us condolences. We had almost as many well-wishers as Johnny's parents.

It was then that Richie looked over at me and said, "So what happens now?"

I had no idea.

CHEYENNE BELLE

It was a guitar pick. I dropped a guitar pick in Johnny's casket.

I had used a Sharpie to write *I love you* on one side and *4ever* on the other. I know. It's corny. But he used

243

to call me Pick, and I needed to do something. For all I know, someone at the funeral home took it out and pocketed it. I thought about leaving him with the gold pick he'd given me at Christmas, but I couldn't. I still wear it around my neck.

Anyway, I had a pretty strong buzz on for the wake, but not strong enough to stop me from feeling every last horrible thing.

The biggest shock was Mrs. McKenna. We all knew that she hated us and hated that Johnny hung out with us, so I couldn't figure out why she acted the way she did. Maybe it was grief. Or maybe she blamed herself for Johnny's death and was, in a kind of way, apologizing. I don't know.

When I couldn't take any more, when I didn't think I could handle one more idiot from Johnny's high school coming up to us and telling us how sorry they were, Jeff walked in. He scanned the room, nodded in our direction, and then went forward to pay his respects. I nudged Harry.

"Please, let's just go, okay?"

Harry saw where I was looking and nodded. He and Richie each took one of my arms, and we left.

When we stepped outside, the night air was cool. It was still March, and spring hadn't really sprung. It was cloudy, and the air was heavy. Johnny's brother, Russell, was leaning against a post, a cigarette in one hand and a book in the other.

Russell had the same curly locks as Johnny, though brown, not blond, and he kept them cut short. He also had the same eyes. They were hard to look at that night.

"Hey, guys," he said, his voice soft. Johnny loved Russell and looked up to him, and Russell loved Johnny back. He was six years older and lived in New York City with his girlfriend. He came to a lot of our gigs, and we got to know him a little bit. We all thought he was pretty cool.

We mumbled hellos and told him how sorry we were, and he told us the same.

Then he held out the book in his hand. It was the little black book Johnny had been writing in for the past few months. The book none of us were allowed to go near, the book none of us, as far as I knew, had ever seen the inside of.

"Here," he said. "My parents gave this to me."

"We can't take this," Harry said.

"I'm not giving it to you," Russell offered with a halfhearted smile, "but I am loaning it to you."

"Loaning it to us?" I asked.

"Don't you guys know what's in here?"

We all shook our heads. Russell fanned the pages so we could see.

"Lyrics. Lots and lots of lyrics. Sometimes with chords written out and sometimes not." I was blown away. "I figure this can be Johnny's final gift to the Scar Boys."

Hearing Russell mention the band was like a slap in the face. I figured that the Scar Boys died with Johnny and didn't give it another thought, you know?

But here was Johnny's brother, telling us something different. I mean, the band was the only thing left holding us together. But how could we go on without Johnny? Wouldn't it be like getting married two days after your husband died?

Like he could read our minds, Russell said, "I think it's what Johnny would've wanted. When you get to the last song in the book, you'll see what I mean."

He handed the book to Harry, hugged each of us in turn, stubbed out his cigarette, and went back inside.

"Diner?" Harry asked, holding up the book.

"Yeah," Richie said, and we piled into Harry's car.

HARBINGER JONES

We probably shouldn't have, but because of what Russell said, we skipped straight to the last page of Johnny's lyrics journal, or at least the last page that had anything written on it. And there it was. The song that would, nine months later, become the Scar Boys' first single:

Everybody said he was such a nice boy,
Always did everything right,

So no one could understand
When the police found Johnny hanging in
the attic that night.

Suzy picked up the newspaper that day.
Headline said, "Local Boy Dies."
She knew her Johnny was gone.
So she took a razor blade and slit
out her own eyes.

Johnny's dead,
Johnny's dead.
Did you see what the newspaper said?
It said, Johnny's dead.

Everyone went to his wake,
Saw him lying there with his guitar.
They all said he tried too hard
To be a rock-and-roll star.

Johnny's dead,
Johnny's dead.

His mother's confined to a bed
Because Johnny's dead.

Now all the parents in the neighborhood
Are acting like they really care,
Just so their little Johnnies
Won't go leaping off the kitchen chair.

Johnny's dead,
Johnny's dead.
Did you see what the newspaper said?
It said, Johnny's dead.

Johnny, that crazy, controlling son of a bitch, had written his own funeral dirge. I read once that Winston Churchill had planned his own funeral—the route the procession was to take through the streets of London, who would speak and who would not, the whole damn thing orchestrated to the last detail from the grave. Johnny's song reminded me of that.

The chords he had written over the words were mostly minor chords, and knowing Johnny, I think he intended us to play it slow, plodding. It took us about five seconds to reject that idea and to give it, to give Johnny, the edge and attitude that both he and the song deserved.

RICHIE MCGILL

It was a fucked-up time when Johnny died. That was the only time I really thought the band was over. I figured we were just cursed.

But Johnny saved us. I mean, he saved the band.

Shit, I don't know. He saved us, *and* he saved the band.

The first thing we did after leaving the diner the night of Johnny's wake was fire Jeff. Harry did it. He called the guy's answering machine from a pay phone and said it pure and simple: "Jeff, it's Harry from the Scar Boys. You're fired."

The dude tried calling us, showing up at Harry's house, coming to gigs, but we always just chased him away. Turns out he really did have some A & R guys at that Irving Plaza gig, and it led to a record deal. Once we started to get successful, Jeff sued us, the freaking wanker. The case is still going on.

Truth is, and no disrespect to the dead, I always thought we were a better band without Johnny, even as far back as that first night in Athens. Everyone thought Johnny was the center of the band, but from where I sat, he was the odd man out. Part of me wonders if he thought that, too, and that's why he, well, you know, did what he did.

But maybe I'm wrong. Maybe Johnny's book is the proof.

The record advance was enough that Cheyenne quit her job, and Harry and I got an apartment in New York City. Chey still lives at home, technically, but she doesn't sleep there a lot. She's living the rock-and-roll life. Harry still worries about her, though. Even when he doesn't tell me he's worried, which is, like, all the fucking time, I can see it. But from where I sit, we gotta let Chey be who she's gonna be.

One of the biggest changes is that Harry has a girlfriend, Thea. She's got something wrong with her face, too. I don't mean that to sound bad; she's actually totally hot, but her chin and the side of her face are all discolored. She says it's a giant birthmark, something called a port-wine stain. I don't know anything about that stuff, but I actually think it makes her look kind of cool. It's like one of Mother Nature's tattoos.

When we started to get popular, we got a lot of people whose faces were fucked up in some way or other turning up at gigs. I mean, they saw Harry as a kind of hero.

Harry, the jerk, was pissed off all the time when he started dating Thea. Some bullshit about how disfigured people should date normal people to prove some point or something. Harry always saw his scars worse than the rest of the world did. Well, worse than I did anyway. Luckily, he got over it, because she's awesome. She's kind of become our unofficial road manager.

As for me, I try not to worry about things. Hell, I'm just happy I get to play the drums every day. I mean, people are paying me to beat on shit. How cool is that?

HARBINGER JONES

I found myself back on Dr. Kenny's couch a week after the wake. I was feeling so messed up that I thought I might explode. Kenny had lost a patient to suicide a couple of years earlier, and I figured he might be able to offer me some perspective.

"That was quite a memorial service," he said. I didn't even realize he'd been there. That was pretty much it for the small talk.

"Harry," Dr. Kenny began, lowering his voice until it was in tune with the Force, making sure I had no choice but to listen. "This is not your fault." He paused. "Do you understand?"

I nodded, but it was a reflex. Of course this was my fault. It was everyone's fault. Johnny needed us, and we'd abandoned him. I could've blamed Jeff and his bullshit "no friendships" rule, and part of me did, but if I was being honest, I knew I was the culprit, I was the bad guy. Johnny told me that first day I'd visited him after we came back from Georgia that he needed me, and I didn't deliver. I was the worst friend in the entire history of friendships.

I'm not sure what Dr. Kenny thought as he watched

me go through those mental calisthenics, but he knew I needed help. He was good like that.

"Harry," he said again, "it's not your fault." He looked me in the eye and did some kind of Svengali thing that stopped me from looking away. I started to cry.

"How can you know that?" I asked. "How can you possibly know that?"

"Because," he answered, his voice weaker than I would have hoped, "at the end of the day, suicide is a choice that is made by someone who is sick, mentally ill, and doesn't have the capacity to choose between life and death. It's an incredible tragedy in part because the victim isn't of sound mind."

"Johnny seemed like a lot of things, Doc, but he didn't seem crazy."

"Depression doesn't mean crazy, Harry. You know that."

"I just don't understand."

"I know, son," he said. He'd never, ever called me son before. It gave me comfort, but in a weird way crossed a line, too. "That's the hardest part. Knowing that you will never understand. Knowing that what you really want, more than anything, is a chance to ask Johnny why, and knowing that you will never get that chance. But sometimes, there isn't a why."

"I can't believe that," I said, wiping the snot on the back of my sleeve. "There has to be a reason."

"Look, there are a thousand reasons Johnny could have been driven to this, but most of the literature, in a case like Johnny's—"

"A case like Johnny's?"

"A suicide that follows a debilitating injury, particularly an amputation."

"Oh." It never occurred to me that there might be precedent for this.

"The literature suggests that Johnny was at greater risk than the average person because of who he was."

Dr. Kenny paused, looking for the right words. I just waited.

"Harry, Johnny was a narcissist. Do you know what that is?"

I nodded. I didn't know the clinical definition at the time, but I looked it up later, and my working understanding—a person with a big ego whose world is defined by himself—was close enough.

"He had such a strong sense of self, of power, of control, that losing it was very hard for him to reconcile. If Johnny had been shy and retiring—"

"Like me."

"Yes, Harry, like you." I always admired Dr. Kenny's honesty. "If Johnny had been a different person, he might have adapted better. But everything about the amputation assaulted Johnny's sense of self. From his surface image to his sexuality to every relationship he'd ever had."

I wasn't really sure I wanted to hear about Johnny's sexuality. It made me think about Cheyenne; it made me wonder how she was feeling.

"Johnny was no longer who he believed himself to be, and he was unable to find any sort of anchor that tethered him to the world. He was literally adrift, unable to hold on to his own identity. In all likelihood, Johnny ended his life because he no longer saw himself as the Johnny McKenna he wanted to be, that he believed himself to be, and that was too much to reconcile."

"But couldn't we have all helped him through that?"

Here, Dr. Kenny paused. A pause with more than enough time for me to fill in the answer to my own question. "A professional could have helped him through it, Harry." He left it at that. He chose not to say what I was thinking, that the people around him, me, Chey, his parents, might have seen the warning signs and pushed him to get help.

The truth is, I have no idea what the truth is, and like Dr. Kenny said, I never really will. But what he said did make a kind of sense. Johnny was the center of his own universe. He had this gravitational pull that seemed to bring everyone else into orbit around him. Not just me and Chey, but everyone. His parents, his teachers, the other kids at school. When he lost his leg, he didn't just lose a physical ability; he lost his gravity. Johnny lost Johnny.

The thought didn't give me peace—it didn't change the fact that I should have been there to help Johnny—but it did give me perspective. I guess that was the most I could ask for.

CHEYENNE BELLE

"Johnny's Dead" was what caught our attention in Johnny's little black book. The guy, such a control freak in life—mostly because his instincts were so crazy good—wrote his own epitaph. That's the word Harry used to describe it. Pretty amazing, you know?

After seeing the lyrics to "Johnny's Dead," I didn't look at the book again for a long time. I couldn't. Harry tried to return it to Russell but was told that it was on extended loan to the band. Russell still owned it, but we would be its keepers. It stayed with us at every rehearsal, at every gig. Harry got a few good songs out of it besides "Johnny's Dead"—"Long Winter," "I Give Up," "Oh So Gray." You know, a hit parade of happy, peppy songs.

Kidding.

Anyway, three months after the wake I was sitting at a gig, waiting for our sound check, quietly nursing a beer, my second since we'd arrived at the bar. I knew I wouldn't have another one before we played, but also knew I'd get plowed the second the set ended. Harry and Richie had gotten used to it, and instead of trying to change me, they just sort of took care of me, looking out for me to make sure I didn't do anything stupid. Johnny's book was there, and I started flipping through it without really looking at it, like a magazine in a doctor's office. As I was flipping, a phrase caught my eye: *To make you think, to make you drink, to make you hurt.*

The song wasn't dated, but it was the last entry before "Johnny's Dead." It said, "Expletive" on the top of the page, which I loved as a title. So I read it.

My heart, which has been broken over and over again, mostly by me, broke for the last time. I finally hit bottom. It was the end.

> *You are a ladybug*
> *On the couch, all curled up,*
> *And I'm like a scientist,*
> *The way in which I insist*
> *You unravel and give all of yourself to me.*

> *You are a little girl,*
> *A flag not yet unfurled,*
> *And I'm like a little boy*
> *With a shiny, sharp new toy,*
> *And I will poke you, and I will prod you.*
> *But you know and I know, I can't make*
> *you undone.*

Is it an empty phrase?
Is it a disguise?
Too long to get through this maze,
Just to say good-bye.

You are a metaphor,
Never meaning the same thing as before.
I am an expletive,
Trying to convince you that I live
Right here, right now, I'm alive.

The more you try to run away,
The harder I will push you to stay,
'Cause the closer that we get
Is one more regret
To make you think, to make you drink,
to make you hurt.

Is it an empty phrase?
Is it a disguise?
Too long to get through this maze,
Just to say good-bye.

Though it's not very long,
It's the end of our song,
'Cause as I look into your heart,
I can see we don't know where to start
With each other, with another.
There's nothing left to say.

I started crying and couldn't stop. Richie saw me and came over, and then Harry. Without me realizing it, they canceled the gig and somehow managed to get me home. Harry's new girlfriend, Thea, held my hand the whole way. It was all a blur.

When I woke up the next day, I was on the couch in Harry's parents' basement, the place where we used to jam before getting time in a real rehearsal studio. I was alone.

"Harry?"

He walked in a minute later and smiled at me.

"Hey," he said, "you feeling better?"

I nodded. "Thanks for getting me here."

"Yeah, no worries."

"What time is it?"

"Around ten, I think. You want to go out and get some breakfast? My treat."

I nodded again. I stood up and started to walk to the

bathroom, then stopped, remembering what had set me off the night before. I froze, my back still to Harry.

"Chey?"

"Harry, did you know about that song?" I asked. He didn't answer at first. "It's okay," I said.

"Yeah, Richie and I both saw it. I wanted to rip it out of the book, but Richie stopped me. Something about a dying man's last words."

I nodded again.

I thought about what those words meant—how we all let ourselves believe there really was nothing left to say. I thought about all the secrets we'd kept from one another, the walls we'd put up between each other, the way we'd all let Johnny just fade away and die. I didn't want that to happen to me.

I turned around.

"Harry," I said. He looked at me, waiting patiently. Always there, always a friend. A friend to the end, you know?

"Harry," I said again, "I think I need help."

EPILOGUE, SEPTEMBER 1991

Scar tissue is stronger than regular tissue.
Realize the strength, move on.

—Henry Rollins

The Scar Boys' first album, *Minus One*, spread like wildfire on college radio, making them the "it band" of 1988. While the record made only one brief appearance on the Billboard charts, debuting and dying at number thirty-seven, the critical acclaim and the growing and rabid fan base positioned the band for the next big step.

Three for the Show, when it was released seven months later, was a breakout success. The band spent a year circumnavigating the globe, drawing crowds in the tens of thousands nearly everywhere they went. That tour spawned their third album, *The Scar Boys: Live in the Shadow of the Heads*.

"It was really just a stupid stunt," Harry tells me when I sit down with the Scar Boys nearly two years after the initial interviews. I catch up with them on a tour stop in Los Angeles, and they are in a playful, energetic mood.

"The few thousand people who live on Easter Island," Harry continues, "had never heard of the Scar Boys and weren't really inclined to like our music. But we wanted to do something grandiose."

The band held a contest, flying one thousand loyal fans to one of the remotest destinations in the world for an exclusive concert in the shadows of the Easter Island heads.

"Man," Richie adds, "that show cost us a shitload of money."

"Yeah," Cheyenne agrees, "but I'd still do it again."

"Why?"

"Because that's what life is about, you know? You have to push the envelope, find the walls of your experience and tolerance, and see what's on the other side."

At the word *tolerance*, I engage Cheyenne about her drinking.

"Sober for eighteen months. Harry's shrink, Dr. Kenny, hooked me up with Sheila."

Cheyenne still likes to make you tease the facts out of her. "And Sheila is?"

"Sheila Carson. She's my shrink. She helped me get into a program, taught me all about how my drinking problem was hereditary, and that I shouldn't beat myself up. It took a while, but it seems to be working. She helped me work through a lot of things."

"Like losing Johnny?"

"Yes."

"And the baby?"

I look at Harry when I ask the question, not sure if he knew about Cheyenne's pregnancy before this whole process began. He catches on right away.

"I've known about the miscarriage, and everything else, since the day Chey asked for help in my parents' basement. We sat and talked for hours."

"What did you think when you heard about the pregnancy? What would Johnny have thought?"

The table goes very silent, and I suspect I've crossed some sort of line. After a long moment, Harry answers.

"I don't know what Johnny would've thought. But if you're suggesting that he wouldn't have taken his own life if he'd known, I don't buy it."

"Me, neither," Richie chimes in. I sense that he's protecting Chey, like a brother protects his little sister.

"As for me," Harry adds, "If I had known at the time, I probably would've asked Chey to marry me."

"Good thing you didn't," Cheyenne answers. We all look at her, waiting for more. "I mean, I would've probably just thrown up on you again." And just like that, the mood at the table is light once more.

I can't help but marvel at how different the bandmates are, how much they've grown. Gone are the innocence and naïveté. Well, maybe not from all of them.

"Check this out," Richie says, somehow managing to stand a spoon straight up in his cup of coffee. The other two roll their eyes.

"How did you do that?" For all the money in the world, it looks like magic to me.

Richie just smiles, snatches the spoon, and takes a sip from his cup.

"What do you think Johnny would make of all this success?" I ask, and everyone is once again quiet, thoughtful. Richie, as is his wont, fills the void.

"Is that a trick question?"

We all look at him.

"I mean, what kind of idiot wouldn't love this life?"

"Richie's right," Harry says. "Johnny would've loved all of this. And he would've made it better. He made everything better." His voice trails off.

"I don't know. I've been thinking about this a lot lately." Cheyenne stares at a point in space as she talks, and I wonder if she still sees that sleeping baby, or maybe Johnny. "I'm not sure he was ever wired to be happy. People with drive like he had need to feel anxious and frustrated; it's what pushes them forward. It's easy for us to blame Johnny's death on him having lost his leg, or whatever, but maybe there was a ticking bomb inside Johnny all along, just waiting for a fuse."

"I don't buy it," Harry says. "There were a million signs for what was coming. I can't speak for anyone else, but I know I ignored them."

"No." Cheyenne counters with enough force to refocus everyone's attention. "We only see those signs now, in hindsight. Everything in the world is clearer when you already know the ending. Sometimes there just isn't any rhyme or reason to the world. It's what makes it so beautiful and so terrifying at the same time."

"Do you miss him?" I ask.

Cheyenne, Harry, and Richie answer without missing a beat.

"Yes." "Of course." "Every day."

After a moment, Harry adds, "Johnny was a victim of circumstance. Really, we're all victims of whatever our own individual circumstances are. For Johnny, it was the idiocy of a drunk driver; for me, it was a group of bullies too young to understand the cruelty of their actions; for Chey, it was having to grapple with the reality of an unexpected pregnancy and miscarriage; for Richie, it was losing his mom when he was a little kid; for you, I'm sure it's something different." Cheyenne and Richie are silent, watching Harry, waiting for him to continue. If there was ever any doubt that he was the leader of this band, it evaporates in this moment.

"Every person on this planet is dealing with their own crap every day. Sometimes we manage it, and sometimes we don't. The way I cope with having lost Johnny is to remember him before he lost his leg, or before losing his leg made him lose himself. It's why I ended that crazy essay I wrote for the University of Scranton where I did, with me and Johnny playing music. I treasure my time with Johnny McKenna and always will. The dude taught me how to be happy."

"Me, too," Cheyenne whispers. "Me, too."

"Is that why you've never replaced him?"

All three bandmates squirm at the question.

"Well, we've had keyboard players touring with us, but

it never felt quite right to count them as actual Scar Boys, you know?" Cheyenne, her scary punk rock girl image intact, stares me down, telling me with her eyes that maybe it's time to drop this line of questioning.

The door to the diner chimes, and Harry's wife, Thea, pregnant with their first child, pokes her head in. "The bus is ready. Time to go, team."

"One last question," I say as they stand to leave. "Tell me what's next for the Scar Boys."

"Same as it's always been," Cheyenne says. "We'll make music."

THE END

ACKNOWLEDGMENTS

I first tried to write the continuation of the story told in *The Scar Boys* immediately after the finished draft of that book was turned into my publisher. By the time I'd reached word number 35,000 of the sequel, I knew I was sitting on something truly, truly awful. My editor at the time, Greg Ferguson, suggested I put it aside and work on something else. Anything else. Not only did I heed his advice, I fully expected that I would never return to these characters again.

But life is unpredictable.

At a Scar Boys pre-pub event at the venerable Anderson's Bookshop in Naperville, IL, one of the attendees, an eighth grade language arts teacher by the name of Wendi Whowell, asked for a quiet sidebar conversation.

"So I have to ask you," she whispered, "at the end of the story, is Cheyenne pregnant?"

"Huh?" I responded.

"Well, she sleeps with Johnny, she throws up on Harry's shoes . . ."

"Oh," I said, paused a beat, and said again, "Oh!"

At that moment, the kernel of the story unfolded in

my brain. People often ask writers where inspiration comes from. In this case it was an eighth grade language arts teacher from suburban Chicago, and I am forever in her debt.

Of course, having the kernel of an idea and writing the book are two different things. I tried a number of different directions before settling on the band interview format, and the manuscript I turned into my editor was . . . unpolished. (I'm being kind to myself here.) Jordan Hamessley, said editor, did a masterful job in guiding me through the process of making *Scar Girl* a much better book. A much, much better book. If you enjoyed this book at all, it's as much thanks to Jordan's editorial eye and skill as anything else. Thank you, thank you, a thousand thank-yous, Jordan.

Thanks also to the entire team at Egmont who was so wonderfully supportive of me. This is bittersweet. By the time you read this, Egmont USA will have shuttered its doors. My time with Egmont was magical. My career as a writer would simply not have started without the hard and brilliant work of not only Jordan and Greg, but also of Andrea Cascardi, Margaret Coffee, Michelle Bayuk, and the entire Egmont team.

Thank you also to Jordan for the *Scar Girl* cover concept, Steve Scott for the design, and the lovely Egmont staffer Cassandra Baim for serving as the model.

Thanks to the entire team at Lerner, the new publisher of both *The Scar Boys* and *Scar Girl*, including Adam Lerner and Alix Reid. I feel fortunate that my work has landed in their skilled care.

Unlike *The Scar Boys*, *Scar Girl* was written on a deadline. This means that there were far fewer early readers. Thank you to my friend and fellow writer Nadine Vassallo and to my wonderful agent Sandra Bond for their feedback.

The parts of the book that deal with Johnny's amputation were informed by a series of conversations with my friend Pat Logan, a prostheticist. When Pat was in his early twenties, he lost his leg in a freak ATV accident. Rather than letting that incident define his life in a negative way, Pat made it define his life in a positive way. He now spends his time and industry in the service of other amputees, and he's one of my heroes. His insight and knowledge allowed me to make Johnny's experience more authentic, and I thank him.

As I did in *The Scar Boys*, I thank my former Woofing Cookies bandmates for their friendship and for our shared experience, and for allowing me to use the lyrics to "Johnny's Dead"—a song we all cowrote in the 1980s—at the end of the book.

A huge thank-you to booksellers and librarians everywhere for embracing *The Scar Boys*. Without that support, this book would not exist.

Thanks to my sons, Charlie and Luke, for putting up with Dad's insane travel schedule in support of his dream to be a writer, and a massive, never-ending, all encompassing thanks to Kristen Gilligan, my wife and partner in all crimes and misdemeanors, for the same. In addition to a lot of weekends watching our kids on her own, Kristen is always my first reader, one of my best editors, and, you know, I love her.

And of course, thanks to my extended network of family and friends for supporting me as you do. I'm one lucky dude.

ABOUT THE AUTHOR

Len Vlahos dropped out of NYU film school at the age of nineteen to go on the road with a touring punk/pop band called Woofing Cookies, which eventually became the backdrop for *The Scar Boys*. He, his wife, and two young sons live in Colorado, where they co-own and work at the Tattered Cover, one of America's leading indie bookstores. You can visit him online at www.lenvlahos.com and follow him on Twitter and Instagram @LenVlahos.